Today new students arrive. The campus is electrified, as if waiting to see what Mother brings home from the hospital.

"I'm glad we don't have to go through that again." Parker points her long, slender hand, Tibetan beads hanging from her ivory wrist, to new students on their way down to the picnic.

"Oh my *God*," Nikki agrees. "I pity them. I mean, look at that little boy in glasses over there by himself. He looks *eight*. Did we stick out like that?"

"Hell, yes," Parker says easily.

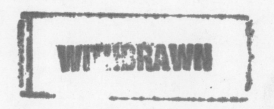

DON'T MISS A SEMESTER . . .

THE UPPER CLASS

MISS EDUCATED

OFF CAMPUS

OFF CAMPUS

AN UPPER CLASS NOVEL

HOBSON BROWN, TAYLOR MATERNE & CAROLINE SAYS

HARPER TEEN

An Imprint of HarperCollins*Publishers*

This book is for our teachers.

1

The Olivettis drive west, into the sunset that wraps New York City in fire. The buildings in the distance gleam with metallic indifference; they're not affected by the cars crawling like insects on the highways and byways around the metropolis. Nikki's in the backseat, biting her maraschino-cherry-red nails, then remembering not to and folding her hands between her thighs, and then biting them again.

"Damn, I'm having déjà vu," she says to Vic and Sharon in the front seat. Her tone is older and kinder than the tone she would have used this time last year, when she thought of them as the enemy.

Sharon catches her stepdaughter's eye in the rearview. "Oh my God, I *swear* I was just thinking that."

"Right?" Nikki answers.

Almost this time last year, they were in the same vehicle, heading in the same direction. Nikki can almost see another white Escalade out the window, its paint reflecting the same wild sunset, and her own self a year younger in the backseat, feet pressed against tinted glass, singing to Green Day, secretly cowering and crying and fighting what was then an unknown future. She can almost see that girl with fear on her bold face.

"How we doing for time?" Vic asks Sharon.

"We're good, babe," she answers.

But Nikki won't return to Wellington Academy until next week; Nikki's taking a red-eye to the West Coast tonight. Sharon and Victor are bringing her first to Anthony's in Queens to eat spaghetti with meatballs, buffalo mozzarella with basil and summer's last juicy tomatoes, and gnocchi with a Gorgonzola sauce.

They pull into the grimy, glittering lot and slam their doors. Sharon runs her hand down Nikki's hair as they walk, asks how she's doing.

They've had an interesting summer, sharing *Us* magazines by the pool and gossiping about Lindsay and Brit and Brad and Angelina, getting their nails done side by side at Lavor salon in the Bradrock mall. They had a couple doozy fights, one when Sharon shrank Nikki's dress in the wash. *I'm not your maid*, Sharon had finally screamed. *I know that now, for fuck's sake,* Nikki had screamed back, and it was a strange compliment.

"I'm *starving,*" Nikki says now. Sharon was giving her an opening to talk, but she's too nervous to take it.

Anthony, who's standing at the phone taking a reservation, steps back, giant hand over his heart, when he sees the Olivettis walk into the restaurant. He's in pinstripes, cheeks red with the sweat of running a restaurant, and his pinkie ring has a chip of sapphire.

"Jesus, Mary," he says now. "Look how you grown up, Nicole."

Vic beams. "Looks like her mother, yeah?"

This is what old friends mean, anyway, when they see Nikki, and are so taken with the resemblance. Vic's friends, like Anthony, had loved Missy, Nikki's mom. Whenever she came in, in her leather trench coat and gold bracelets, they seated her so the whole restaurant could see her. But a year ago Vic would have avoided a mention of her no matter how much fancy footwork it required.

Nikki smiles at her father. So bizarre that leaving her family last year has brought them all closer together.

She's never flown alone, and stands nervously in line, gold sandals and white duffel on the conveyor with the string-tied pastry box in which Anthony put her "cannoli for the road." Her parents wave, blowing kisses.

"Love you, princess," her dad calls, and everyone in line turns.

The plane pulls onto a night tarmac. It's an empowering feeling, once they're amid stars, the wing's light winking: *I am on my own.* She squishes the pillow against the porthole, and closes her eyes.

Pictures Seth. Every minute suspended over the nation's slumbering cities and lakes and hills, she gets closer to him.

Closer to him. She opens her eyes. She hasn't slept. They've only been in the air for a half hour. Nikki's unable to push away the possibility she's been stifling since she bought this goddamn ticket. She reviews phone calls and e-mails, conversations between her and Seth, nuances, or hesitations.

What if this trip is a disaster?

Maybe he'll introduce her to some girl who's tolerating Nikki's visit but has been with Seth all summer. Seth's family will hate her. Or Seth will stop fooling around with her the first night and say: *I was hoping this would feel right after all this time, but I hate to say it, Nik, it's gone. Let's just spend the rest of the trip as friends, cool?*

Nikki stares at the universe, where planets spin and stars shoot, where the air is thin, too high for birds, too late for warmth, too far from home, and too close to California.

She feels like a doormat for coming back to him.

Vanessa asked her twice if she was sure she should visit him, after what occurred—implying that Nikki was accepting bad treatment. The real nucleus of her fear is "the viewing room"—her code for what happened last December. The last time she kissed Seth. The first time she had sex. The only thing that came close to breaking her heart after losing her mother—after believing that her heart was permanently broken and so could not be broken again.

He fucked up. He knows it, he's written an apology, he's made apologies over the phone, sober, drunk, high. It's a ritual: the "I'm so sorry, Nik" phone call.

She's explained what hurt most: *I thought you were so emotional because it was amazing. And then I realized you were shaking because you were angry. And the thirty seconds it took me to figure that out, while you were talking, Seth, was as painful as watching you draw an Exacto knife down my hand. It was just brutal. Do you understand?*

I understand.

Are you sure?

Nikki, I swear to God, I'm sorry. I swear to you.

Nikki turns off the light and draws the shade. She has only seen Seth once since he left school. They met in Central Park one Sunday when Seth drove down from his grandfather's house in Maine to see Nikki, and she took a train from Wellington—three hours each way. They sat under flowering trees and said nothing, shoulders pressed together, petals twirling down from the branches and landing in their hair and on their faces and in their laps.

She wakes up, light streaming into the porthole, her neck cramped. It's dawn. She looks down and sees diamond water and palm groves. The office buildings of downtown San Diego. Houses, aquamarine pools.

We're landing.

Seth is meeting her at baggage claim. Nikki twirls her long dark hair, waiting in the yellow halter and cutoff jean skirt Vanessa helped her pick out, hoop earrings, gold sandals.

He's got to love me. I'll effing make *him love me.*

The escalators roll up and down like riddles. An alarm goes off. A belt lurches into motion, debuting luggage through the fringe.

"Yo," he says.

She spins around. "What's up, stranger," she says with a grin, most charming when she's terrified.

"You're finally here," he says, and runs his hand through the long black hair that falls over one eye. He looks at her with a crooked smile, hands plunged into the pockets of his jeans.

She drops her bag, holds out her arms. "Aren't you going to hug me, asshole?"

He laughs and gives her an awkward hug. When they

part, they both search the other's face, with no conclusions.

They walk to the parking garage, holding hands, her duffel over his shoulder. Palms flutter in slow motion in the balmy breeze. The sky is miraculous.

"I can't believe you're in my town, I get to show you around," he says.

"I know, I'm so psyched," she says, neither of them able yet to relax and say anything remotely original.

"This is me," he says, and drops her duffel into the trunk of a black Mazda. Nikki likes the Cali plates, and how it feels to be in the passenger seat as he zooms onto the highway. Below is sugar-white sand and obsidian rock that juts into the surf. He points out landmarks and neighborhoods. This is where he was born and raised. The salt is in his blood. Shifting the stick, he flicks his eyes over to her. She smiles. As they drive she keeps one hand on his shoulder, feels the muscles work whenever he changes gears.

His house is stucco, hedged in with hibiscus. Simple homes line the block; there's a relative sense of affluence, of parents who work, of kids who go to college, of once-a-week housekeepers, if not live-in help, of Jeep Cherokees and almost-new Volvos, if not Range Rovers and BMWs.

It's Monday, and no one's here. In the foyer, Seth finally takes her face in his hands and kisses her. Nikki sneaks a look at them in the mirror. His forearm, his sunglasses on Croakies, the T-shirt, dark blue jeans. *I didn't dream him up. This kid exists.*

"How you feeling, Nik?"

Good question, I don't effing know. The house is empty and so ready for them. Nikki is not ready for the empty house. They might have talked about what happened the day of "the viewing room," but they have never revisited each other's bodies, the real crime scene, the heartbreak's location.

So she presses her cheek to his chest and murmurs that she's tired. "But I want to go swimming," she says, pulling away to look at him.

"Let's go swimming, then."

They change and make a pitcher of iced tea. Nikki clambers onto a raft and Seth takes the other, and they drift, eyes closed, toes and fingertips submerged, rafts gently colliding. Even though she's nervous and ecstatic, she fades in and out of sleep. He splashes her, and she shields herself, splashing him back. They chitchat about what to do this week, and then fade into turquoise daydream, spinning, floating.

It's not till they get to his favorite burger place, perched on a boardwalk above the surf, when they start to really talk. They sit under an umbrella, eat fries swaddled in waxed paper. They squint at surfers who carve lines down the sapphire waves.

"Not bad, right?" he asks as they bask under the big sky.

She smiles at him. "Not bad at all."

The fact that he was kicked out of school, that she had been involved, that he hurt her so badly when he left, in "the viewing room"—all of this is a black spot on the sun. For now they talk about summer, which is safer.

"Yeah, it's been weird, because a couple of my buddies aren't going to school this year," Seth says, dragging fries through mustard. "They don't want to hear about September. Although they put it in everyone's face that they'll be working and partying, all year-round. Whatever. To each his own."

"You could have had to stay with them," she reminds him.

"Christ, tell me about it," he says, smiling darkly. Three colleges withdrew their offers after Seth was drop-kicked from Wellington. "So weird, that at the end of the day, I really don't need to stick around this joint. Used to think that would be rad."

"I hear you," Nikki says. She's slumped in her chair, slurping Diet Coke. "It's like toothpaste from the tube, you know what I mean? You get squeezed out of your home-town, no problem, but it's impossible to get back in."

"Yeah, yeah," he says in his ominous manner, using the tine of a fork to etch meaningless symbols in the ketchup.

She remembers what an up-and-down guy he is. "You're going to love New York," she says.

He looks up, eyes hopeful under the glossy cascade of

hair. "Right? I feel like I am. Yesterday, I went online to find record stores. Dude, there's a hundred. It's insane."

"I think you're meant to be there," she says definitively.

"Shit, where else would I be, though?" he asks with bitter humor. "Hunter's the only place that didn't rescind."

Gulls cry. The birds coast on wind, their shadows hovering on Nikki and Seth.

After a silence, Seth asks: "How's your, uh, stuff with Vanessa?"

She loves when he tries to be a boyfriend and talk about her life; he's so awkward. "The same," she says, shrugging. "I don't know. Like, things get better sometimes, we'll be tighter, and then I say something about Wellington, or *you*, or Parker, and she gets so cold. She makes sure I know how much I missed this past year. You know what I mean?"

"I do, I do," he says with happy unhappiness: *trademark Seth.*

She punches his arm. "You're so morose," she says, laughing.

They stroll down the steps from the café, tropical bushes growing on each side, and he reaches for her hand. She could walk down these steps forever, stoned on sunshine.

They pass the aquarium, and he practically blushes as he points out his summer job. But she *likes* to think of him in his La Jolla Aquarium uniform. He wore a name tag and snipped admission tickets in the blue room where sharks would slide sexually against the glass, meeting the pane with a muted bump. Stingrays fly, their wings rippling. Redfish gleam like pennies. Kids lick ice-cream cones and leave trails of hardening drops on the floor that look like confetti.

He squeezes her hand. Maybe he's still in love with her.

They're giggling, rolling around on the bed in the room where Nikki's staying, when Seth sits up. He puts his finger to his lips and jams both beer bottles into her closet. He motions for her Altoids. Then he slips out the door, pantomiming to stay put.

Christ, he's got me freaked out.

She was *already* nervous about meeting his parents, not sure whether she got tied to his expulsion. She looks in the mirror, smoothes her turquoise halter dress.

She hears Seth say: "She was just unpacking and getting settled, I think. Let me see if she's ready."

"Come meet my folks," he calls to her.

Seth's parents are going through the mail, briefcases on the floor.

"Well, hello," his mom, Tina, says. "How wonderful to finally meet you."

"Great to meet *you*," Nikki says, offering her sweating hand.

His dad, Craig, shakes her hand too. "Welcome, so happy you're here."

"Thanks. It's awesome to be here, it's so gorgeous," she blusters. "I love it."

They're California people: athletic and balanced and healthy and mellow. They ask Nikki about her flight. They ask how her summer has been going.

"Great, great," Nikki says.

If Seth was at her table, her parents would bully him—in their New York way. *Come on,* they'd say, gesturing, eating, and talking. *Spill the beans. Whatcha been up to? Give us the details, here.*

"I hope you're hungry, Nikki," Craig says.

Dinner is a Mediterranean salad with grilled chicken, flatbread, and lemonade. At only one point do Tina and Craig act weird. Seth says he's taking Nikki to a bonfire party later in the week, where she can meet Delia Breton. Both parents stop eating.

"Are you sure?" his dad asks.

Seth gives them don't-be-stupid eyes. "Yeah, I'm sure. What's the problem?"

"No problem," his mom says.

"They're both going to be at Wellington," Seth says.

Nikki assumes the issue is the party. "We won't stay out late," she ventures. "I'll probably still be jet-lagged anyway."

Then both parents change their tune and smile. "I'm

sure you guys will have fun," Craig says.

After dinner, Seth twirls his car keys and talks about taking Nikki to the movies.

Craig, with his handsome smile, says, "Why don't you just stick around tonight, okay? Watch a movie here."

Seth seems deflated, drops his keys in the junk basket.

So they all sit in the den, and Tina brews ginger tea. When *Riding Giants* is over, the parents yawn. They make it clear everyone is supposed to go to bed, and Nikki gets up. She thanks them for dinner, and Seth says he'll show her the extra blankets, and anything else she could need during the night. She blushes.

"You should have everything here," he says, pointing to towels and soap on her bed.

"Cool, thanks," she says.

As he says good night at her door, he gives her a kiss that means she won't be able to sleep. But he steps away and walks to his own room.

All night, Nikki imagines his footsteps. But he never arrives. Suddenly Nikki has the idea that he's ashamed of what he did in "the viewing room" and is projecting it on Nikki's body. It makes her cringe in the sheets.

She's in his sister's room, whose pictures are everywhere. Celeste, Nikki's age, is dark-haired, small, mischievous. Nikki recognizes her public-school glare: the look her friends at home still share. In the photographs she's tan, hair shiny with Jamaican braids, with rope bracelets on her strong arms. This summer she's on a NOLS trip in Maine, sleeping under cold stars while this other girl sleeps in her bed.

Nikki has to pee but is afraid to be seen in her black nightie by a parent. *Why didn't I bring wholesome pajamas? This isn't the honeymoon suite.* She feels like a dirty magazine accidentally placed on the children's shelf in the library. Her airplane fears come back—that he doesn't want this, that it will never be what it was. The sun eventually spills through the slits in the blinds, slicing into the dark.

She gets up after the parents leave for work, and she and Seth eat in the kitchen. She's got a sweatshirt on over her negligee. Seth makes coffee, his hair sticking up, shirtless in sweatpants. He scratches his hard stomach as the coffee percolates.

When he puts down their mugs, he smiles at her. "Do you want sugar, Nik? It's in that bowl, there."

She watches him cut a grapefruit. She realizes that she's upset. Nikki's not ready to jump into being physical, but she's hurt by him not trying. He doesn't want her.

"Um, how do I say this?" he starts.

Nikki looks at him, fear in her eyes like a cat's pupils at night. "What?" she asks in a dead tone.

"I just feel like, I don't know," he starts again, without

looking at her face.

"Seth, just say it," she says.

"I think it's a good idea for us to wait to, you know," he spits out, studying his mug. "It's worth it."

It's worth it. Such an abstract statement, but she'd have it tattooed across her heart using a safety pin. It's better than *I'm sorry*, or *I owe you this*, or even *I love you*. Because it means Seth cares about this future.

"Thanks," she says, smiling shyly.

And this is better than *I forgive you*, or *You're right*, or *I love you too*. Because it means she'll move on, that they're heading to the same place. Suddenly her grapefruit half looks like a jewel. And she eats it, and looks at the black lace of her nightgown against her thigh, and her red toenails, and she feels the half of herself that will do anything to be loved, and the half of herself that hates the half of herself that will do anything to be loved, suddenly welded together.

This is how broken hearts are repaired.

2

She meets Delia Breton the third day she's in La Jolla.
Delia's reputation precedes her like smoke before a fire;
the way Seth says her name means she's formidable.

Nikki and Seth are bantering like they did at Wellington, the dirty baby talk, the mock wrestling. But they
haven't crossed any lines.

Today he brings her to Black's Beach without telling her
it's a nude beach. He walks down like it's nothing, leaving
Nikki to stare, bug-eyed, at naked sunbathers on the gilded
sand. They bought sandwiches and sodas, but Nikki whispers that she can't eat here.

"Why?" he asks.

"Are you *kidding*? Look at that man's balls! They're practically in my face!"

Seth laughs. He pretends he's about to take off his shorts, and Nikki looks at him, horrified. "What are you *doing*?" she asks.

"Aren't you going to get comfortable?" he asks.

When she fumbles with her bikini's clasp, he takes both her hands. "I'm kidding, Nik. Totally messing with you. Let's walk down the beach. I was just playing."

She laughs for him, and they walk into the burning sun, and Nikki realizes that she's *still* not a hundred percent ready. His joke didn't feel great. She doesn't want to feel played, not if it has to do with her body.

When they settle in their new spot, he tells her about the bonfire that night. "That girl Delia, who's going to Wellington this year? We're going to pick her up and bring her."

"Cool," Nikki says. "Are she and Celeste best friends?"

"Naw. They used to be friends, but they're not tight anymore, I don't think."

"Why?"

Seth shrugs, lifting his sunglasses to rub sunscreen on his nose. "I don't know. I guess she's a handful."

I like her already.

It's four when Seth and Nikki head over to Delia's house. They pull up a drive lined with palms. A group stands in front of the Spanish mission–style house. A girl with stringy dark-yellow hair does slow curves on a long-board skateboard. The guys are older, and Nikki gets but-terflies.

"Get out of my way, dick!" the girl yells, laughing hoarsely, an ice-cream cone dripping down her hand.

"Go *around*, you retard," one guy says lazily, leaning against a lime-green MG so old and rusted it looks like it might disintegrate.

Seth introduces everyone: Delia, and Turner and Mason, her brothers, who are dark-blond like their sister, and Charlie, a friend, who's olive-skinned with a black Mohawk.

"What's up? How you doing? Welcome to La Jolla, babes," Delia says, licking the melting vanilla ice cream from her hand to shake Nikki's. "Dude, I'm so gross! Sorry. That ice-cream truck guy, he's kind of hot. I eat ice cream, like, night and day."

"She's a friggin' mess, dude," Turner says in a surfer-boy drawl, shaking Nikki's hand.

"It's totally cool," Nikki says, already enchanted by all of them.

They head inside so Delia can get her things, and come upon Casey, the mother, making guacamole, squeezing limes into chopped avocado. She squeals, wipes her hands on a dishrag.

"Well, hello, Nikki. I've heard all about you. I'm *so* glad to meet you, and so glad our Delia will have a buddy. She'll be far from home, and we're going to miss her so much."

Casey has brown button eyes, a runner's body, and a California-girl smile. Nikki blushes from the maternal affection. As they chat and wait for Delia, who's getting ready upstairs, Nikki surveys the kitchen. She decides she wants to live with the Bretons.

Herbs and jalapeños hang, drying, from the pot racks. Copper pans simmer on the stove. Cats drip off the counters, like drops of cream, silent. Surfboards lean against the porch screen, and wet suits dry on a whitewashed wall outside. Flowers and cactus plants grow in glazed pots and hanging macramé planters. Aloe vera spears tower near the sink. Joan Baez plays from an old stereo.

"So you got there last year?" Casey asks, a hand on her hip. "How do you like it?"

"I mean, it's got its ups and downs, you know? If I was at home–"

"Where's home, honey?"

"Long Island. If I was there, my life, it would be so different. The school at home is decent, but Wellington is crazy. The library alone has more materials than any library I've ever been to. I can't complain. I've made some really good friends." Nikki's too proud to admit the school has some *serious* drawbacks. She can't admit that she made some really good enemies there too.

Casey stares at Nikki, nodding. "That's phenomenal, Nikki, I'm so happy for you. I am." Casey makes that sound genuine. "Which dormitory are you in, Nikki?

Delia's in Gray, on the first floor."

"Awesome. I'm in Gray too, on the third floor. All the Upper-forms and seniors live together at Wellington."

A white lab, yellowed like scrimshaw with age, limps into the room, and Casey kneels to kiss her. "And God, Nikki, any advice on what she should pack, besides the basics? We've been stacking things up in her room for a month now. But I just feel like we're missing something."

"Well, just make sure she has warm stuff, good sweaters. I don't think I brought enough when I first went up there."

Delia bounds down the stairs, in terry cloth shorts and a yellow T-shirt, gold bangles, no shoes. No makeup. Just her dark tan and flower-child beach-bum hair. She tastes the sauce on the stove, and Nikki sees that her left hand is covered in a red birthmark like drops of paint.

"That's good, Ma. What is it?"

"Bouillabaisse. Ben's coming over with his daughter."

Delia glares. "He's not bringing his daughter."

"What should he do, Delia, leave her at home?" Casey says sharply, and glances apologetically at Seth and Nikki.

Delia shrugs and smiles meanly. "Yeah."

As Casey gets ready to hash this out, Delia waves at Nikki and Seth. "Come on, let's go," she says.

No home is completely perfect, Nikki thinks.

Casey stands in the doorway. "Be careful, you guys. Seth, drive carefully, sweetie. Nikki, I loved meeting you. We're just so happy Delia knows someone before she gets there. We know it's uncommon to transfer in as a junior . . . excuse me, Upper-form."

"Jesus. Enough, Mom." Delia pulls Nikki's arm.

In the car, Delia sits crammed in the backseat, and leans up to talk. She fills space like a superhero. Her hair lies on Nikki's shoulder. When Nikki says she loves her perfume, Delia reaches into the unicorn Jordache bag and pulls out Ralph by Ralph Lauren.

"I don't know what the hell it is, I stole it from my friend," she says.

Nikki laughs, and sprays it under her arm. "I stink," she explains.

It's Delia's turn to laugh. "Seth," she barks from the backseat, where she's now decadently leaning back, arms spread up behind her. "I like your girlfriend."

The party is fun. On Long Island, the closest thing would be some gasoline fire in a parking lot, bass thumping from a car, doors open like hawk's wings. People sharing 40s and Lynchburg Lemonade, until there's a fight. *Your guy got too close to my girl. You're looking at me funny. You're a whore. You're an asshole.*

Here, there's beer, a joint sizzling from mouth to mouth in the sunset darkness—and s'mores. Delia jumps, dancing and shouting to 50 Cent, riling people up under the moon, and that's it. No one flashes the handle of something tucked into the waist of their Nautica jeans. No one keys anyone else's car.

Seth and Nikki spend the night with arms around each other, as embers float like backward stars.

She feels shy around these Californians. One lesson she learned at Wellington last year was to never take lightly the difference between herself and other people. She'll never walk into a new scene as cavalierly as she did Wellington. Seth's friends stand with them for a few moments at a time, chests stuck out, visor lids red from fire, board shorts starched with salt. Nikki answers their polite questions, but mainly she stays starstruck by this other coast.

"You okay, baby?" Seth murmurs into her neck.

She nods lazily, happily.

She can't help watching Delia. With her wide face, coarse hair streaked blond and dark brown underneath. Delia jumps from group to group, making noise, hugging people around the waist. Like the world's kid sister.

When they say their good-byes, Delia begs them to stay. "Oh my God, I can't believe you're leaving! Oh shit! Listen, Seth, you got to give me her number. Nik, I'm going to call you right before school starts. Holy shit, we're going to have a blast."

They hug like they've known each other ten years.

On their way to the car, they pass a crew of beach gangsters whose arms are smooth and sculpted like *Playgirl* models, bleached hair glowing in the San Diego night. "I think you have a girl-crush on Delia," Seth singsongs, and Nikki punches his chest, laughing.

Delia sleeps in a room on the third floor, and from her window she can almost see Mexico. Down in the yard, her aunt's strange sculptures of angels and tigers and naked men stand among jasmine. There's a feeder of red sugarwater for hummingbirds.

But hummingbirds don't come at night. Demons do.

Delia lies in bed, and her demon is who it most often is: herself. *Was I too loud tonight? Did that girl Nikki think I was a freak? Was I really forward with her? What was everyone at the bonfire thinking about me being there? Did they say things to each other I couldn't hear?*

She smoked pot, and it makes her paranoid. Her own soul is her ghost, and she sees herself jumping in the dark around the bed, making sure she can't sleep. She dances around the imaginary bonfire, ash marks on her terry cloth shorts, and perfume on her skin, and that look on her face she knows she had all night: *I love every one of you and need you desperately; please don't come near me.*

Nikki has to credit Seth, because he plays his cards with his parents, and with her. They mess around on the twilit beach, in his room, they kiss in his pool, they hold hands walking through downtown La Jolla, looking at tan, freckled, rich people in paradise. But they don't go too far.

Until the night before she leaves, when they go to a party in a mansion overlooking La Jolla Cove. It's his best buddy, Steve Norrin, and Steve's parents let the party go till 3 A.M., drinking at their own friends' house across the street. Nikki and Seth stand around, sipping Budweisers, dancing to Sublime and Peter Tosh and the Killers, passing a marble pipe jammed with purple hydro, lounging on sofas covered in fern-print fabric.

Nikki takes a picture with her phone from the front porch: a diamond bay, simmering in moonlight.

"Where you been, Nik?" Seth asks when she comes inside.

"Nowhere."

He kisses her head. "I just called my folks, told them I couldn't drive, and the Norrins are letting us stay here."

Nikki pulls away. "Are you serious?"

He nods, triumph on his face.

"You were a good boy all week, just so you could get points to spend the last night. And they went for it," she surmises.

"And guess what? We're taking the guesthouse. Care of Steve."

The guesthouse is also the pool house, and its rooms,

wallpapered in a seashell print, smell of chlorine. It is a scent she will forever associate with love.

As opposed to what happened in "the viewing room," this time it goes slow, and easily, and seems to be all about her. Anytime she tries, he moves her hand.

"No, it's my turn." And he keeps asking her: "Does this feel okay?"

She feels like telling him that he's not a doctor and she's not a patient but she likes too much that he's caring about her.

"Yes," she whispers instead.

It doesn't hurt, and he doesn't get up afterward. He kisses her hot neck. Rolls off her eventually, gets a towel, and comes back to hold her. They don't sleep, because each time he comforts her after, one of them gets ready again. By the time the pool house windows are milky-gray with morning, Seth and Nikki are spent and exhausted and sore. Nikki lies there, dazed with euphoria, and watches a June bug on the wall, its perfect antennae shivering as it crawls. She's too tired and ecstatic to think it anything but beautiful.

"I don't want to leave," she says.

"I don't want you to leave," he says.

And there, in the guest cottage, under a baby-pink chandelier, in sheets damp with ocean air, the Pacific roiling and churning a hundred feet away, they make their vows.

"So we're going to do this?" Seth is afraid to meet her eyes.

She smiles and reaches for his face. "Yes."

He kisses her and lays his head on her stomach. "So no other bitches, huh?" Seth bites her stomach and rolls over to look at her.

She laughs with him. "No, you loser. No other bitches."

It's settled. They're going to be committed this year, long-distance. They belong to each other.

3

The new Wellington year begins. The school is cracked open like an egg. BMWs and Volvos and Land Rovers are parked on the lawns in front of dorms, their back doors lifted to freshly washed linens and milk crates of books and computers and vintage Mark Cross duffels. Parents make polite hellos to each other, and they make sad good-byes to their kids.

"What's up, playa?" a kid in madras shorts says.

"Chilling. How you been?" The two guys slap hands, smile slyly as if this is the year they're going to slam-dunk.

"Yee-*ha*," growls Brenda Fahey. She's a stout, tough girl from Michigan, a softball legend, and her friends flock to her like puppies, all of them in Umbros and jog bras under college T-shirts.

Parker, Nikki, Noah, and Greg got here yesterday and are enjoying the last day of summer on Parker's great-aunt's quilt on Rooster Hill. The day is plump and golden, like a fruit about to bust. Most returning students are already here, straggling in from their hometowns, pinning up tapestries in new rooms. They're connecting one by one.

And today new students arrive. The campus is electrified, as if waiting to see what Mother brings home from the hospital.

"I'm glad we don't have to go through that again." Parker points her long, slender hand, Tibetan beads hanging from her ivory wrist, to new students on their way down to the picnic.

"Oh my *God*," Nikki agrees. "I pity them. I mean, look at that little boy in glasses over there by himself. He looks *eight*. Did we stick out like that?"

"Hell, yes," Parker says easily.

For returning students, orientation blows air through stale halls. A new crop means another chance at a best friend, a bigger crew, a new crush, a better hook-up. The returning students feel the hierarchy of the school shifting. New cliques take over prime cafeteria tables, and kids who swung from tighty-whiteys on the flagpole last year are this fall's monster-hazers. *The meek shall inherit the school.* The unofficial understudies of the star seniors, who graduated last year, come out on stage, blinking in the spotlight.

Summer gossip crystallizes into legend: *Did you hear about Fielding getting kicked out of Windridge for hooking up with a camper? Dude, what about Jill Lassiter? She's not coming back. She wrecked her mom's Audi, crashed into Shinnecock's gazebo. Her parents chucked her in rehab just so they wouldn't get thrown out of the club. Martin Helbridge's mom committed suicide; he found her in the garden shed. His uncle took him to Cairo, and he's still there.*

Greg and Noah sprawl on the country-plaid-and-floral quilt. All afternoon they've been studying the Facebook, which arrived in mailboxes like an early Christmas gift.

"Have we identified her yet?" Greg points to a Lower-form girl from San Sebastián, Spain.

"Roger that. False alarm. She must have Photoshopped herself."

"You guys are evil sometimes," Parker says lazily.

She's lying back, one hand shielding her face from the sun. A sliver of stomach shows between her worn olive Carhartts and CBGB T-shirt, and Nikki catches the guys looking. Noah shakes his head. They're both thinking the same thing: *Chase really blew it.*

"Yo, who's *that*?" Greg points to a blonde from La Jolla on the next page.

"You mean Delia?" Nikki asks.

"You know her?" Noah asks.

"Yeah, I met her when I was out there with Seth. She's

a friend of his sister's."

"Shit, hook me up." Greg rips out blades of grass and tosses them at Nikki.

"Not sure she goes for meatheads." Nikki winks at Greg in his varsity football T-shirt. "Especially ones with fight scars."

Everyone laughs. Greg has a claw mark on his neck from a fight at a baseball game in his park in Brooklyn. He'd been drinking, and Greg cannot hold even a thimbleful of liquor.

"All right, all right, whatever," he says, rolling his eyes.

"But if I *do* hook you up, you better return the favor," Nikki kids him.

"You on the market, Nik?" Noah asks, surprised.

She's known this would come up. But everything that happened with Seth last week is too fresh and too precious to talk about with these guys. After a pause, she proceeds with bravado, and checks out her nails: "Maybe."

"How about you, Park?" Noah asks.

"Off. Officially," Parker deadpans.

Nikki laughs.

"It's not that funny." Parker stares at Nikki.

"I know, sorry, it's just how you said it."

Nikki heard about Parker's summer. She and her hometown guy, Peter, road-tripped to Vancouver with his alt-country band, The Poor Harvests. Parker was their roadie-slash-groupie-slash-manager. They traveled in an orange Winnebago Peter bought for five hundred dollars. They ate Ramen and PB&Js the entire trip, and showered at trucker rest stops when the Winnebago got rank.

Peter wrote songs for Parker and sang them at honky-tonks or college bars. They slept in the same single bunk, listening to the sounds of unknown towns, woken up by strange birds.

When Parker returned home in August, her parents said an unexpected guest had dropped by on a road trip of his own: a Southern kid named Chase. They told him Parker was with Peter. They insisted Chase stay the night, but Chase just thanked them and asked them to please tell Parker he stopped by.

Parker still hasn't seen Chase Dobbs since last year, and this accounts for the way she seems to be hovering, like a body in a séance, a few inches above the quilt. Parker's back at school, but dreaming, living the summer over so she doesn't have to confront the autumn.

Nikki likes her new room with Parker, in Gray. They're on the third floor, overlooking the golf course's slopes through a Japanese maple with violet leaves. The building's walls heat up as electricity runs through cold wires. Water's flushed through the old pipes. The place is awakening. The housemaster on Gray One is an art teacher, Mrs. Jenkins.

Her marmalade cat sits in the tree, lazily looking down on girls entering and exiting the dormitory. Parker stands at the sill and makes kissing noises until he looks up, disdainfully.

"He's like the Cheshire Cat in Wonderland," she says to Nikki.

They have a lemon-yellow butterfly chair, Italian movie posters with beautiful people kissing or riding motorcycles, and 1980s record albums pinned to the walls. Schuyler Covington is no longer a citizen of this world. Nikki languishes on her bed, an autumn breeze coming through the window. Parker catches up with Laine, who's popped in to say hi. Laine's playing Varsity Field Hockey again, and she's fresh from practice, grass bits plastered to shin guards, cheeks red.

"I mean, did you and Miss Hartford talk about, like, *everything* that went down?" Parker asks.

Laine shrugs. "Yeah. It is what it is."

"I hear you," Parker says, legs crossed Indian-style in the butterfly chair, braiding strands of her long hair. "At least the team isn't so toxic this year."

"Exactly," Laine says.

Nikki was nervous to see both girls, not for any reason, but she was shaking when she hugged them hello yesterday. Parker is more confident this September, but also closed, as if the price of her morale was shutting out society. And

Laine looks good, her blond hair cut into a bob, her face not as skeletal, her stride not as uncertain as after she fell to pieces. She's *still* an arm's length away, and yet she's here, which is what matters.

What amazed Nikki was how bonded she felt to these two girls. Like they'd pricked fingers and mingled blood and were transformed to sisters. They'd seen one another's bad sides, the peaks and the nadirs, and they'd seen one another in love. They'd seen one another lose. They'd fallen down and helped one another up. They had changed one another.

"I'll catch you girls later," Laine says as she leaves to shower.

"We should make the most of the rest of this day, Nik," Parker says, looking at the sun. "It's back to the grindstone tomorrow."

They pass orientation groups sitting in circles by the Science building. They're dappled by the copper light of the Connecticut afternoon. Everyone wears Wellington T-shirts, still creased from being folded in welcome bags—not unlike the kids themselves, who look freshly unpacked from their old lives.

"There's that girl, Park, that I told you about." Nikki points at Delia: board shorts and a faded blue Sector Nine skateboarding shirt. "Oh, poor thing, her leader is *Linden*. He's probably going to make them group-hug any second.

We should rescue her."

Nikki and Parker hide behind a tree trunk and make hand gestures at Delia. New students in the group turn with that scared bunny-rabbit look that Nikki had a year ago. *I can't believe I'm on the other side of things now.*

Delia jumps up. She runs over and hugs Nikki, who basks in the attention coming from the orientation groups.

Nikki motions at Linden. "Hey, Lin. Do you mind if we steal her for one second? She's got a phone call."

He's on the cusp of objecting.

"You rule, Linden," Nikki gushes, linking Delia's arm with hers. "I'll bring her back in one piece, I promise."

The three girls walk fast in the direction of the dorm, giggling. Nikki introduces Parker with a flourish of her arm.

"Great to meet you, Parker," Delia says.

"Same here. Cool shirt. You skate?" Parker asks.

"Just long-board. But it's actually not mine. I teafed it from one of my brothers when he was like eleven."

Nikki insists they head to the rope swing. "Greg said the guys are going down there. Delia, you have to see this place."

Parker looks away as if thinking. "You know, I really can't. I've got to finish unpacking. But you guys go."

Nikki suspects Parker is scared of running into Chase, but she doesn't push because she kind of wants Delia to herself; it will be like showing off a new toy. Parker moves away, and there's a heartbeat when Nikki could say: *Let's just chill in the dorm then,* or *Come on, Park, we'll go down there together.* But instead she lets her friend slip off, and swings Delia around like a Rockette, their arms linked.

Nikki and Delia walk through the woods, sun melting through the emerald canopy into the darkness. This place is strange, and Delia's already overwhelmed. She's ecstatic from foreign sounds and fragrances, atmospheres, the contours of the dorm, the light spiking through treetops onto the soft-needle floor, and this girl, with her Juicy shirt, gold necklaces that hang in her cleavage, this girl who's small-town suburban *and* worldly, gauche with a raw accent and dismissive eyes, but tender too. This girl, Nikki, who knows her way through these woods.

"So are you and Seth, like, what's your deal?" Delia asks. "You guys aren't going to be totally monogamous, are you?"

Nikki holds a branch from the path for Delia. She shrugs, purses her lips as if this is old hat to her. "I don't know. We'll see, right?"

"I mean, you guys will have really different years."

"Yeah, totally," Nikki says as if she has it all figured out. She changes the subject, and breaks down the guy situation they're about to walk into. "I should warn you, Chase Dobbs is a player. I'm not into him, but for some reason two of my best friends have been."

"Yeah? What's he like?"

"Well, he used to have long blond hair—kind of surfer style, but he shaved it at the end of last year."

"A surfer boy? Don't worry. I have those at home."

"He's a typical prep school kid, you'll see. If you're not *from* this world, it takes a while to get his appeal. I was, like, *lost* when I arrived. But anyway, Chase is in the middle of some kind of evolution or whatever."

"Celeste said it didn't take long for Seth to trade his Quicksilver for Patagonia."

"Ex-*act*-ly." Nikki smiles. "Then you have Greg Jenson. He's from Brooklyn, and he's such a good guy. Football. He gets pissed sometimes, and can be, like, way out of control. But otherwise he's awesome."

Nikki and Delia stop in a clearing when they see the boys from a distance.

Brand-new people, Delia thinks.

Chase and Greg are shirtless, standing on a steep bank, peering down into the lake. Chase is holding the rope, tied to the limb of a giant oak. The boys look mystical, not quite solid—a projection in the humidity.

"That's Chase," Nikki says quietly. "And that's Greg."

Delia stares.

"Hey, guys. What's up?" Nikki calls out.

"Hey, Nik. 'Bout time you showed up." Greg's talking to

Nikki, but looking at Delia.

"What's up, Nik?" Chase's crew cut has grown, his body tan and lean from working at the Sullivan's Island docks.

"Guys, this is Delia. She's a new Upper-form, and she's friends with Seth from California."

"What's happening, Delia? I'm Greg."

Greg holds out a fist, and Delia bumps it. His sapphire basketball shorts glimmer in the deep woods shadows. She finds it almost impossible to look at Greg's black-bronze shoulders, his chest—she looks instead at the ground, where flip-flops and big Adidas sneakers are collected, the sneakers' hollows glittering with a gold Zippo, a Skoal tin, a key. She looks at Greg's ankles, spangled with pine needles.

"I'm Chase." Chase gives a half-assed wave.

"You going to stand there with that rope between your legs or are you going to do something with it?" Nikki asks with a wink.

"I'm waiting for *Gabe* to get out of the way." Chase stares down the steep bank.

Nikki looks, expecting to see chubby Gabriel Velez. But the guy clambering up the bank is someone else. The summer burned off all the baby fat; Gabriel is crystal-sharp. His face is precise, brown eyes big above cheekbones. His arms are lean. He smiles, aware of Nikki's surprise.

"Good to see you, Nik." He kisses her on both cheeks.

"Here we go." Chase leaps onto the rope. "Yippee-ki-yay,

motherfuckers!" he hollers. He soars twenty feet above the water and cannonballs.

"That looks awesome," Delia murmurs, and steals a glance at Greg. When he looks at her, she looks away.

"So, are you and Chase roommates this year?" Nikki asks Gabriel.

"No. They split us up. Chase is in Summer. Greg, Noah, and I are in Eliot. It sucks for him. It's Siberia down there."

"Chase, my man, thanks for swinging the rope back," Greg scoffs. "That kid is on some sort of solo trip right now." Greg scrambles down the steep bank, grabs the rope, and hikes back up.

"Can I take a turn?" Delia asks when he gets to the top.

"Oh yeah. No doubt."

Greg hands Delia the rope. She feels the fibers splinter into her fingers, and she grips and re-grips the rope, tries the perch with her bare feet. Then she jumps out, swings higher than Chase did. Suspended above a green mirror. But the rush is after she's let go of the rope and before she touches water.

Splash. She opens her eyes down there, for one moment, in a void.

She breaks the surface, she's laughing. "Oh my God, that's cold!"

Everyone looks at the girl who treads water like she was born to swim.

* * *

In the showers on Gray One, Delia washes off lake water and silt, tastes it in her mouth as it runs down her face. So different from Pacific brine. She can summon the aroma of kelp, wet stone, sand, ocean. Her wide, brown feet are splayed on the white tiles. *How did I get here?* Every single tile is brand-new; she feels the newness of this place with molecular intensity.

"Hey there," a girl says to Delia as she pads barefoot in her towel back to her room.

"Hey." Delia smiles.

The girls on her floor seem nice, their faces portraits of different worlds. An Asian girl is taping a poster of a cellist onto her wall. Two white city girls stand in a room, one fixing a chain on the other's neck with Avril blaring in the background. A black girl in an orange DON'T MESS WITH TEXAS T-shirt does push-ups while someone Delia can't see talks, eventually making the cornrowed girl laugh so hard she collapses on the floor. Peeking into each room, Delia checks out floormates as if they hold clues, the way one reads a book's chapter titles to know how the book ends.

Perhaps she can really start over here. Delia stands in front of the mirror. She tries a comb through her hair. The shade is down, and light comes through the brown parchment like burnt vanilla. Fear starts in her belly. Delia remembers her mother's voice: *You didn't do anything wrong, baby girl. People are stupid, they like to talk. Just get away from here, Delia Ba-delia, and you'll be fine.*

Delia liked that turquoise void. She liked coming up for air and seeing Greg. He'd been watching to make sure she wasn't drowning. He winked and turned away. Almost shy. *God, there's just something about him.*

4

And so the year begins, lurching into motion like a rusty machine just oiled. Everyone compares schedules, buys books, labels notebooks. Upper-form year, as teachers tell it, is the most important year of your life. College acceptance is based on how you do this year, and in a school where students compete against one another to take the few spots each Ivy allots a single prep school, the year is intense from day one till they pack up in May.

Nikki sits at the round table in Poli Sci 213. Rain trickles down the windows, and the raindrops' shadows trickle down the room. Ms. Westerhouse, a young teacher two years out of Yale, is introducing the semester's focus: contemporary Central American governments. The class glances at Gabriel.

What's he thinking? Nikki stares across the room. *I mean, here's a kid who has literally* lived *this, and he's not saying a thing.*

Even students who can barely locate Colombia on a map know that Gabriel's father is the Treasurer. He's in the news, a stoic figure in grainy photographs whose morality is contested by some and celebrated by others. Nikki's heard the story. Gabriel's family rose to power through coffee, and Gabriel's father extended their influence into the political world. Last year, Noah and Nikki Googled him in the library, and there were hundreds of articles and even a few fervent books devoted to him. One photograph shows Señor Velez in a blue serge suit, his black hair glinting, shaking hands with a bishop, whose brocade gown barely lives up to Señor Velez's elegance.

But for a kid with so much, why is Gabriel so soft-spoken?

She's always thought of him as Chase's roommate or the Colombian politician's kid, but he's changed, he's come into himself. He looks like his father. Nikki wonders what his life at Wellington has been like. She heard the rumors. How a couple of olive-skinned campus security guards with accents showed up when Gabriel arrived. *Maybe he's here to get away from Colombia.*

In Mal Pais last spring, he was like a cousin, a brother, a comfort, a host. She thinks now of those tropical nights, brilliant days, and she can't remember a single conversation with Gabriel. She recalls sitting on her chaise longue, baking, geckos darting from hibiscus to hibiscus, and she knows Gabriel said things, but she can't remember one word.

"Nicole, what do you think?" Ms. Westerhouse asks.

"Sorry, I'm just . . . Could you repeat it?"

"Weren't you listening?"

Shit, first day of class. This isn't good.

Gabriel shoots his hand up in the air, and Ms. Westerhouse's eyes light up.

"Yes, Gabriel."

"I don't think that's *totally* true. Both U.S. operations were in response to the Cold War. But look at their outcomes. I mean, think of all the U.S. troops currently fighting the same Afghan rebels their military fathers supported. I don't see that happening in El Salvador right now."

Nikki mouths, "Thank you." He smiles and returns a "You're welcome."

The shadow of the rain trickles over the globe in the corner, tears spilling over the continents and oceans.

Delia walks across the grounds on her third day of school. This is a storybook place, a collection of buildings that seems too grand and ancient to be real. The grounds seem miniature even though they're big. After the dunes and beach and sky of California, New England is tiny and cramped, its woods small and dense. The buildings are warrens. The days are short, and the nights are dark.

"Hey there, Deals," some guy says, using a nickname he obviously feels comfortable using.

"Hey," she answers.

The people here, as opposed to Californians, are turned inward. They stroll aggressively. Their talk is studded with code words: *Quogue, Fifth Ave, Fishers Island, Bedford.* They're like big actors on a tiny stage. They're entitled to everything. The dress code is coats and ties or turtlenecks for guys, and the abstract equivalents for girls. This population is buttoned up.

Delia's not homesick, exactly. She sometimes feels, especially as the day gets grayer toward evening, a heaviness. She pictures her heart crammed with sand and jasmine and gray water. She remembers the exact taste of an In-N-Out burger. She can trace with her hand the slope of her dog's back, the way his spine has gotten knobby and distinct in old age. She can feel her mother's fingers taking Delia's thick hair, twirling it around her wrist, saying, *Look at that, look at that rope.*

She likes soccer, which is where she's headed. She knew she'd make Varsity, and she did. And she likes the field, the grass crisp and dying, the brisk air that keeps body temperatures down. This is better than playing in California. All her life, she and her brothers spent afternoons kicking the ball around the yard in bathing suits, wearing black DC sneakers, Public Enemy blaring on the radio, sweating.

Delia's more comfortable out here than in the dorm—that hotel of possible gossipers. Hearsay doesn't make it to the playing fields. Girls are purest on the turf; they look one another in the eye, they pass, they shoot. They win, they lose.

Although in the showers, one girl mentions Greg to another girl, and Delia almost falls over trying to hear. They all know Greg, she realizes. It's a small school. The girls are standing under nozzles, both shampooing their hair, eyes closed. Bubbles slide down the black girl's skin as she shakes her head slowly with appreciation.

"That kid is fine."

The white girl tilts her face to the water. "He's in my Spanish 413. Just watching him roll those *R*'s, yum."

Delia's at her locker. It's funny: Out on the field, under the sky, playing a game with these girls, she felt no competition. But now that the game is over, the game has just begun.

Nikki's old advisor, Mr. Murdock, had been an introverted ceramics instructor who couldn't even relate to his own daughters. When Nikki came crying to him after Dean Talliworth told her to stop dressing "promiscuously," Mr. Murdock accidentally knocked a vase off his desk. This summer, Seth suggested switching to *his* old advisor, Patrick Somerset.

Seth told Delia the same thing. Delia and Nikki meet on the steps of Gray. Nikki's wearing skinny jeans and a violet DKNY jacket. Delia's in a big Irish knit sweater that belonged to her mom and faded Levi's.

"Hey, babe," Nikki says. "How you holding up?"

Delia grins. She assumes Nikki refers to the transition any new student would be making. "Not too bad, Ma. Everything's good."

They tromp over twilit-wet grass. Nikki loves the way Delia's hair takes hours to dry, the tips blond, the roots wet and dark. She grabs Nikki's arm or hand to emphasize a point. Delia skips sideways, talking to Nikki, acting out her stories.

Delia brings up Greg. "These two girls kept *talking* about him, and I felt like, *Hey, ladies. Nuh-uh. Back off.*"

"You gotta get there first, girl," Nikki says.

They ring Mr. Somerset's bell.

"Come on in, you guys," he says.

Mr. Somerset's living room is packed with advisees for "meet and greet" pizza night. The leather couch, the fly-fishing photographs magneted to the fridge, and the New Orleans Jazz Fest posters scream "bachelor," as do his flannel Beretta shirt and frayed Levi's. He's lanky, with mussed honey-yellow hair. He isn't handsome, his nose is too long, but there's a warmth and easiness to him. Delia thinks he's like a boy who was forced to grow up, who wears his adulthood apologetically, as if he betrayed or abandoned these kids.

"Welcome, welcome," he says when everyone's seated. "Welcome to my humble abode."

Besides a couple preps and Lower-forms, there's a Saudi Arabian senior named Malkeet, and a PG, Luke Rediker, from Bend, Oregon. Greg mentioned to Nikki that Luke needs grade massaging before playing Division One ball—and that he smokes mountains of weed.

"Sorry, guys, if I knew Luke was showing up, I would have ordered three more pies," Somerset begins. "Let's keep this casual. I know how painful orientation can be. I was at Taft not too, too long ago. So, I want you to feel if you have a problem—and it doesn't have to be academic—I'm here. Any questions?"

"Could you define 'too, too long ago'?" Delia asks, sitting Indian-style on the floor.

"Go look it up on my Facebook page. Does that help?" Everyone laughs.

Delia's gaze lingers on him as people line up with paper plates. He reminds her of this guy who worked at her friend Mara's farm near Big Sur. She and Mara were eleven and had a crush; he must have been seventeen or eighteen. He washed up in the artichoke fields with a backpack, dirty jeans, and expensive sunglasses, and worked the summer. Looking back, he probably had a trust fund, but he was picking artichokes under the broiling sky, afternoon after afternoon. Mara and Delia would hide in the plants and watch, his golden back straining as he harvested. He left in October, to keep looking for some world he could abide. He was beautiful *because* he was lost.

Somerset feels Delia's attention, and he looks at her. She shakes her head, smiles, and he winks, turns back to the crowd.

They watch *Weeds*, while Luke finishes off a liter of Coke and an entire pizza. Toward the end of the night, Delia challenges him to a belching contest, and Luke burps and silences the crowd.

"All right, that's it," Somerset says. "Luke, you owe me some incense, and next time, no pepperoni. Class dismissed!"

They walk into the night, and moths are carousing in the cones of light from the path's lamps. The moths won't survive the first freeze, at midnight tonight. They seem to know it, the way they flutter against one another.

Delia sets her alarm. She lies in bed with the lights on. On her wall is a vintage poster for an old California train line. The engine passes straight through an orange grove, the trees heavy with fruit. A farmer and his dog watch the machine pass through their cultivated Eden. The poster is reflected in the black window behind Delia, and Delia and the window and the poster are reflected in the glass on the poster.

She wakes up suddenly, as if tilting dangerously on a wave. She breathes, scared, and touches the sheets. It's a bed. It's a room. And in the building are rooms and rooms of girls.

She can't tell if these girls are friends or enemies. Her mom swears that if you act confident, you are confident. If you feel beautiful, you become beautiful. *Whatever, Miss California Sunshine.* But Delia can't quite refute this truth. Did she bring dishonor to the East Coast? Did she invite the girls to exclude her? It's not even that they've snubbed her. There's a chill in the air, but it might be that Delia herself is bringing that chill.

How do you lift your head up after you've taken a fall? She shuts off her lights again. Her mind falls back to an afternoon when she was nine. Her brothers and their friends were skating in the Buzzard Beach lot, someone's car playing Eminem. Will, the eldest, the invincible, was fifteen then, and could do sharper tricks than anyone. The sun lit his curls like a crown. He hit the ramp, and his board floated under his Chucks as he soared. He smashed down, his face meeting asphalt, his hands sliding like meat on a grater. Everyone stood silently, boards in hand, and waited. Will got up. It took a long time, and he moved like a broken robot. He got back on his board and did one slow lap while everyone watched. When he came near his little sister, she stared at his face. Diamonds of glass were embedded in his lip, his eyes were wet, and he held his head high.

Nikki calls Seth. It's strange to dial a 212 number and hear his voice. She imagines his window, looking out to hundreds of other windows, the starless New York City sky bearing witness on its millions of citizens. Yellow taxis blurring in the streets. A fire engine screaming. Cleaning people making their way through cold, desolate offices. Bartenders cutting lemons. A junkie making a scene in a church garden, sending birds into the air in wild compassion. This is where Seth lives. She imagines his face reflected, pale blue, in the glass of his window, dissolving into Manhattan.

"Yeah, what else?" he asks.

"Um, we went to Somerset's for pizza."

They talk about nothing, in sweet, low voices. Around them is still the wreath of chlorine mist that was in the pool cottage. The pink chandelier still glimmers. The June bug's antennae still move spastically, and the insect makes its shadow on the eternal wall.

5

It happens faster than it ever has for either of them with anyone else. Nikki and Delia are best friends by the second week of school.

They're hanging out in Delia's single, which they call the Penthouse Suite, since it's rare for an Upper-form to live alone. It's a blue Sunday, and they're playing her iPod and tearing pages from *Vanity Fair.* They feel glamorous, by virtue of hanging out and excluding everyone else.

"I'm *bored.*" Delia is facedown on her pillow while Nikki inspects her closet.

"Just wait. In a few weeks there'll be *so* much drama at this place. It just needs time to develop." Nikki catches her wise veteran tone and cuts it short.

"Where's Gabe and *Greg?*" Delia singsongs, and then

pops up to see if she's piqued Nikki's interest.

"Why? Who's on your mind?" Nikki teases as she slips off her T-shirt and slides on a tunic. "Cute. Can I?"

Delia shrugs and stands up. "I think Greg is *sexy*. He's got that *man* thing happening. His body is ridiculous. Gabe's definitely not bad either."

Nikki nods without meeting Delia's eyes. She's been having trouble explaining Seth. She said something about monogamy the other day. Delia thought she was joking: *Can you imagine if you really did that? You tried to be loyal to someone who you never saw for a year?*

Nikki's flattered that Delia *needs* her to like Gabriel so they can go after the guys together. Old-fashioned soda-fountain double-dating. Delia seems terrified of doing it on her own. If Nikki passes on it, Delia might find a new best friend.

And Nikki feels prim about her oath. Like a Little Bo Peep with a Bible in her hands. A Little Miss I-Shall-Not. A teenage nun. *What would be so wrong with kissing someone if Seth never knew? It's not even dating, it's just having a social life.*

Delia and Nikki sit on her desk, blowing smoke through the window fan.

They begin that conversation all new girlfriends must have.

"Are you a virgin?" Nikki asks Delia.

Delia shakes her head, rueful, proud. And so they begin trading the facts of their lives as tokens of trust, like wampum beads.

"I was twelve when I gave my first hand-job," Delia says. "I did it so wrong, he had to ask me to stop."

"I got naked with this guy when I was thirteen," Nikki offers. "We were swimming. We didn't really do anything, because I thought you could get pregnant just from being near it in the pool. His parents came home, and I grabbed my clothes and ran into the garage. That night, I was watching TV, and my dad looks at the bottom of my feet, 'cause I was, like, lying on the couch. They were totally black. I picked up all the oil from the garage floor."

"I did it when I was fourteen," Delia says. "Oh my God, it hurt so bad. Afterward I cried and cried. Holy shit, he didn't know what to do. I just sat there in this bedroom, we were at a party, and we were in the little brother's room. There were toy trucks and stuffed animals everywhere. This guy was so worried, he sat there with his arm over my shoulder, but it was super awkward. He had a big gold chain on his neck, and a tattoo of Donald Duck on his shoulder, 'cause his brother was in Iraq or something, and his name was Donald. Anyway, this moment lasted for *years*, dude. And then he offered me some gum."

"No way!" Nikki says. "You're not serious."

"Bubblicious, watermelon. Like that was going to make everything okay. There's, like, blood on this little kid's racing-flag sheets."

"So what'd you do?"

"I took the gum."

The girls fall over laughing.

"Yeah, I gave my first hand-job in a limo, with two other couples," Nikki says. "So retarded. We'd been drinking like Belvedere and Red Bull or some shit. I did it through the fabric, like, through his rental tux. And we had to stop because we were going through the White Castle drive-through, and it's this *nerd* we all know at the delivery window."

Delia claps. "Get out!"

And then Nikki tells Delia about losing her virginity. How Seth met her in the library viewing room. The carpet. How he wanted to, how he asked, and put on a condom. He was shaking. She was shaking. It was nothing like what she'd imagined. What she'd dreamed was seamless. Something that didn't hurt.

"I hear you."

And then she explains that Seth had just been told he was being kicked out. "So it was a good-bye. How twisted is that?"

"Oh, baby," Delia says. "I'm sorry, but that *was* twisted."

"He made it up to me this summer," Nikki says shyly.

Delia's face is serious. "Good. He should have."

They're silent for a spell.

"Do you like it here, at least? I wanted to kill myself this time last year," Nikki says.

"If it weren't for you, I'd go insane. I mean, I like your friends, but I don't really know them yet. I miss the California weather. And my *mom*." Delia suddenly grimaces and looks away.

"What was that?" Nikki says sharply.

"What?"

"Why did you give me that look and then look away?"

"I didn't mean to." Delia stares at her friend. "It's just, I know your mom died so I felt, like, awkward complaining about mine. I'm sorry."

Nikki stares at the floor. She takes a last drag, crushes the butt in a Diet Coke can. "Whatever."

Nikki feels Delia looking but won't meet her eyes.

"Hey," Delia prods. "I'm sorry."

Nikki shrugs, smoothes her jeans on her thighs as if about to get up, but she doesn't move.

"Nik. I won't make you talk about it, but I'm a good listener. I've had a few fucked-up things happen in my life. I'm not saying I know what you went through. But you can definitely try me out."

Nikki smiles bitterly. She wants to make a joke, pull it together, stop showing all her cards. But she's paralyzed.

"What was her name?" Delia asks quietly.

Nikki finally flicks her eyes at Delia and then away. "Missy."

"When did she die?"

"On a Friday. When I was twelve."

"Were you guys tight?"

Nikki tells Delia stories about her mom, stories from

before Nikki was born, and after, and right at the end. Stories her dad told her, about Missy trying to learn piano but never graduating from the basic melody of "In a New York Minute," which was the only song she wanted to learn anyway. Of how she baked cakes when she was sad, three or four cakes at a time, and then had to give them to neighbors because the Olivettis couldn't eat them all. How she took Nikki pumpkin-picking, the October before she died, even though they'd never done that before, it's not like it was a tradition, but Missy wanted to do things with her daughter. She tramped around that field in a wig, heels sinking into the dirt, and she and Nikki laughed so hard they sat down in an aisle between vines, the Long Island sun sinking and turning the white rabbit fur of Nikki's jacket gold.

And later, when Nikki thinks about Delia's broad face and open eyes, how she listened to every word—she realizes Parker has never asked about her mother. Laine made an attempt, but it was more of an acknowledgment. Missy has been standing there, in her gauzy dress on the threshold, waiting to be invited back into her own daughter's life. Delia saw that and opened the door for the beautiful ghost.

"Yo, Deals, got a dollar to spare? I need a Coke, I'm fucking falling asleep," Chase says.

He's caught up to her in the hall between classes. And

he does look exhausted, his flaxen hair flat and unwashed, his eyes dull.

"Of course," she says, digs in her backpack.

But a lot of Upper-forms look exhausted. The work seems infinite, multiplying in the darkness of a desk drawer, within the pages of a textbook, like a virus. The Upper-forms clomp through marble halls, bug-eyed on Ritalin and Red Bull. There's not a lot of connecting; people talk to each other like automatons and move on. Delia wonders, for example, if she'll ever get to know Chase, who's just taken her dollar, thanked her, and walked off.

"Bye," she says, as he disappears through the stone arch of Cranberry Hall.

And there, down the end of the hall, is Greg. Playing hackey-sack with an eraser. His leg, in black slacks, keeping the pink cube in the air. He catches it as Chase arrives. Chase says something to him, and Greg looks down the long hall. Makes a small wave in Delia's direction, but she can't tell if it's for her. He shrugs and turns away, and then she knows it was. But it's too late. The boys vanish in the light of the arched tunnel.

Maybe he's touched something off in her. Walking through the music wing and passing glassed-in practice rooms, the glass triggers a vision. The memory never comes back in one piece; it's like postcards of the event that get sent to her one by one. Split-second images of that bad day.

The glass. The blue eyes. *I'm thirsty.*

Then Gerald tells Rachel: *Why don't you go get some orange juice.*

The glass door gets locked.

The towel.

The glass door, unlocked, swings open.

Delia has stopped walking and is standing in the corridor. The muffled violin from one room, and the scales someone's singing in another room intersect here. Delia's at the crossroads of an unearthly duet.

The college advisors hold a meeting for Upper-forms in the auditorium. Everyone slouches, blowing bubbles, sucking Snooz, acting tough in the face of unknown futures and rejections. They put their loafers on the seats in front of them, practicing their *I didn't want to get into Brown anyway* postures. Delia looks everywhere for Greg, but he's not there. Football takes him out of many after-school obligations.

"We have SAT workshops every day, in the admissions wing," Mr. Gerry is saying. "Come down. If you don't take the initiative, we can't do it for you."

Afterward, Delia looks dazed. "Dude, I just got here, and they're telling me to get ready for the next place. I mean, *chill.* Come on."

Walking into brisk dusk, Delia's and Nikki's hair gets blown by blustery wind. Dead leaves spiral in blue shadows. They link arms.

Nikki leans conspiratorially to talk into Delia's ear. "Listen. We'll get in somewhere, we'll go somewhere fun. They act like this is the end of the world. It's not. It will be what we make it."

Delia nods. "Tell it, sister." Whether Nikki's right or not isn't important.

In her psych class today, Delia looked at Rorschach tests. She thinks of her and Nikki as two sides of an inkblot. Each other's reverse in most respects, but the same shape. Two wings. Put them together and fly away.

It's Saturday night. So far the year has been a mad scramble, and everyone in Upper-form missed the first Saturday night because they got slammed with work and games. There's been no flirting, playing. Nikki saw a documentary about a women's prison across a field from a men's facility. The men and women would sign a homemade language through the electric fences, desperate for interaction, courtship, sex.

Parker's doing Nikki's makeup while Delia watches.

"Oh!" Nikki says. "I have the craziest shit." Taped under her desk is a bottle whose label reads RUSH.

"What the fuck is that?" Delia holds it. "Dude, this is *ether*."

"My friend Ness gave it to me."

"Smells *nasty*," Parker says, dabbing Nikki's lips with a

wand of ice-pink gloss.

"You drink it?" Delia asks.

"No. Just sniff it for like two seconds. Watch." Nikki unscrews the top. She holds it under her nose and whiffs. She hands it back to Delia. "You try."

Delia watches Nikki's head slump a bit, an angelic look on her face. Nikki giggles, eyes closed. Delia sniffs. She sees tiny silver balls. *Holy shit, this is great. This is great.* It takes her to heaven. Then slowly fades, and she comes back.

Nikki grins, talks thickly. "Sick, right?"

Delia laughs. "God*damn*."

Nikki holds it to Parker. "Here, sweetie."

Parker smiles, waves it away. "I'm good."

There's silence as the girls register their dynamics. Delia and Nikki feel bonded for being illicit, and small for being declined by Parker.

"Your choice," Nikki says haughtily.

Delia looks at Parker. "I don't blame you, this stuff is gnarly."

But Parker doesn't look at either of them.

Delia's more dressed tonight than Nikki's ever seen her. Dark blue jeans, a turquoise shirt, gold hoops that almost touch her shoulders. California bohemian. Nikki thinks she knows why.

"You finally going to talk to Greg tonight?" she asks coyly.

Delia shrugs shyly, and smiles. "Shit, I gotta."

"You guys would be awesome together," Parker says. "He's a cool kid."

"So, what do you think of Gabe, Nik?" Delia says.

"I love Gabe. You wouldn't have recognized him from last year. He was like this cute, pudgy Latin kid. Now he looks like a movie star."

"So why don't you try something with him?" Delia asks.

Nikki shrugs. "I don't know. I mean, he's beautiful."

"He's beautiful," Parker agrees.

Everyone uses this word with him. He's prettier than he's supposed to be, his features mythical, romantic.

"And so?" Delia prods.

Nikki looks at her. "He's too nice or something."

"You want someone who will treat you bad?" Delia asks.

That's not quite it. "It's just that I like really strong guys. You know what I mean? But I hate not having someone. Someone to chase at least."

All three girls have been raised to be complete, to know that they don't *need* to be someone's girlfriend to matter. Their mothers helped pave the golden path to self-sufficiency and financial power and new etiquette. And yet Nikki, Parker, and Delia can relate to cheerleading bobby-socked girly-girls from fifty years ago, who at age seventeen cared for nothing besides boys.

"Then you should chase Somerset." Delia breaks the silence.

"Oh, come on, *Somerset?*" Nikki says, not totally sure Delia's kidding. "I don't *think* so."

Parker steps back to survey her work. "Somerset? He loves checking girls out, I swear."

"I saw you looking at him," Delia says to Nikki. "He's not bad for an older dude."

"Ew, you sound like the slut from *American Beauty,*" Nikki scoffs.

Delia gives Nikki a sultry look: "*There is nothing worse than being ordinary, is there?*"

"Let's go. We are *not* ordinary." Nikki throws an arm over Delia's shoulders.

"Hold on, I'm not ready," Parker says.

"Who you after?" Delia asks her.

Parker surveys her closet, pulls out a violet coat. "No one," she answers without turning around.

Nikki shakes her head at Delia to keep her from continuing.

Always got to put my foot in my mouth, Delia thinks. She could be on a desert island with Nikki and it would be a party, but with Parker, she still doesn't know what to say. The girl *seems* cool, with her top hats and silver nail polish and pink leopard jeans. Her art books and old-school Walkman. But closed off.

"You got to talk to him someday," Nikki says to Parker as they walk down the stairs.

Parker gives Nikki a deadly glare. "No, I don't, actually."

Delia recoils, having started this.

The student center is filling up as people arrive from the movie, and voices are high, rambunctious. The guys are congregated near the pool table, sipping Vitaminwaters and eating grilled cheeses off greasy paper plates.

"Girls." Chase nods his head at Parker, Nikki, and Delia as he prepares to break.

His eyes are glassy, Greg's grin is goofy, and Gabriel's silent.

"Smells like the boys had some fun, too," Delia says under her breath as they find a booth.

Nikki can feel Parker's discomfort. At some point, she has to get over this. So far, she and Chase have just pretended like the other is invisible, and it makes everyone uneasy. Nikki sits angled away from Parker, annoyed. *She's such a quitter.*

Nikki hates that she and Parker are the old maids here. Nikki hates being on the sidelines. Who knows what Seth is even doing right now? She's not one to sit out; she was a monster at board games her whole life, collecting chips and fake money, and making fun of losers. In charades, if her *own* team sucked, they heard about it. She played video games with the guys, her legs splayed on a cigarette-burned carpet in someone's basement, twisting the joystick, her strawberry-glossed lips cursing at the boys and with the boys. She cursed if she lost, and cursed with glory if she won. Nikki didn't play to win, she just played to play.

"By the time this game is over," Nikki says aggressively to Delia, "you will go up and talk to him."

"Come *on*," Delia protests, toying with a straw wrapper.

"Listen, everything happens fast here, when it happens at all. You'll see."

The girls share fries, lounging as if they have nothing on their minds. Nikki feels the guys looking. Greg comes over and asks for one. Delia looks at him with childlike eyes.

"Heard you tore shit up on the field today, Delia," he says, licking ketchup off his thumb.

"Oh yeah? Thanks," she says, and hides the birthmark on her hand.

Parker spends the time looking out the window. No moon. Delia and Nikki watch the guys play, talking over Parker's silence.

Nikki juts her chin at Greg, who's watching Chase sink the eight ball. "Go."

Delia grits her teeth. Nikki nudges her out of the booth, and Delia stands up awkwardly.

"Jesus, I'm going to faint," Delia looks back to say as she walks over to Greg.

She and Greg stand in the corner and talk, and Nikki watches them, smiling as if she made the match. Delia keeps her hand in her back pocket, and Greg seems nervous too, touching the stubble on his chin.

"What do you think?" she asks Parker.

Parker gives her an odd smile. "About what?"

Nikki suddenly feels wrong about her impatience with Parker. She looks at her friend, her hair brushed out and gleaming on her vintage white sweater. The makeup she'd done on herself, copying a picture from *Annie Hall*. She's wearing a fake ruby ring she got out of a machine at the supermarket. She's all dressed up with nowhere to go.

"You want to head back to the dorm? Go watch bad TV and eat whatever's left in the vending machine?"

Parker's smile changes into something sadder, but relieved. "Yes, please," she quips like a kindergartner.

As they pass Greg and Delia, Delia makes a don't-you-dare-leave-me face, and Nikki wiggles her fingers at the couple. "Ta-ta!"

It's not long after that Greg looks at the ceiling, seeming to summon his courage. "Place is pretty stale, right?"

Delia knows what she's supposed to do but is not sure she can. Finally, she manages: "A little bit. You want to take a walk, then?"

Greg nods and grabs her hand as they slide off the shelf where they're sitting.

The glass door to the game room swings open and Chase looks over at them. He laughs at their intertwined fingers.

"What?" Greg says belligerently.

Chase shrugs, turns away, hits a ball that jumps the wall and lands on the floor, violently bouncing away. "Nothing."

As Greg and Delia shuffle down the corridor, Chase leaps onto the couch and holds his hands to his mouth like a megaphone: "Ladies and gentlemen, there he goes: The captain of the football team and certified player, Greg Jenson, is leaving the building. Show some appreciation." Chase begins clapping and the students follow suit.

"Jealous asshole," Greg says under his breath with a sheepish grin.

The chapel floor is cold on Delia's back, her T-shirt pushed up. Greg moves, his breath a mixture of Sour Patch Kids and Aristocrat vodka. She tries to be quiet, the big silence in the chapel is daunting, crushing. She runs her hands along his waistline, over his chest and along his back. She can feel him as he moves faster. His mesh shorts rough against her thong.

He rolls off her and sighs in frustration and restraint and desire. *"Damn."*

"I know. Maybe sometime when we aren't in God's house and we have more than eight minutes."

He runs his hands on her skin, closes his eyes. "Please, let's not talk about God right now."

She laughs and grabs his hands, although she's so nervous

her own hands are shivering. "We don't have to talk about anything," she whispers.

And they lie like that, touching but not moving, staring at the gilded ceiling. Delia's where she wants to be, from the first minute she saw him by the lake. It's like Greg was waiting for her to get here. They're together. For some reason, Delia is always more comfortable at first with a guy in the dark than in the bright, social rooms of daytime life.

Seth and Nikki talk on the phone. It's late, but Seth is about to go out. Nikki imagines his door, the elevator, the grimy, loud sidewalk outside his building. Girls and guys in ragged furs and glittery makeup and spike heels, smoking, laughing raucously as they walk to the next party from the last party. She imagines Seth blocking the cold with one shoulder, strutting through the crowd, that swath of black hair in his eye.

"What else?" she asks him.

"Oh, shit, I failed this surprise quiz in my film class. And I *like* the class, I just wasn't ready."

They talk in their low, resonant phone voices, rehashing their days and nights for each other, and meaning something else. You can't say *I miss you* over and over; that's no conversation. So they talk the detritus of mornings and afternoons, hours and incidents. All Nikki wants is to feel the heat of his mouth on her, and what she gets is a cold electronic device.

Seth looks out his window. His face is superimposed, blue and eerie and beautiful, on the city. But his features, in Nikki's mind, are smudged, like an overdeveloped photograph. The stars of the city skyline are burning him away.

6

The next day, Delia and Nikki take the roundabout route to Somerset's apartment while Delia talks fast and crazily about Greg. Delia tries to contain herself for fear of bragging, but she's too excited. They trudge in the woods, sharing a cigarette.

"It was amazing," Delia keeps saying. "I felt like I knew him, you know what I mean?"

"Completely."

"I mean, we didn't do much. But it was really natural."

"Totally," Nikki says, trying to suppress jealousy.

"Anyway," Delia says, as if sensing this. "Greg said Gabe talks about you all the time."

"*Really?*"

"He's a bit obsessed."

"*Really?*"

Somerset swings open the door. "Come on in. Come on in." He stares down the corridor and sees no one. "You're a little late. We barely have enough time to get through the episode." Somerset sits in a worn suede recliner. He pushes back the sleeves of his houndstooth jacket. "But I'm glad you made it."

"Yeah, sorry," Nikki says in a self-important manner, as both girls are energized by being the only ones invited over. Maybe their hypothesizing about Somerset's crush on them isn't wrong. The girls trade I-told-you-so looks: *He wants us.*

And the theme song plays: *Little boxes on the hillside, little boxes made of ticky-tacky . . .*

Minutes into the show, Somerset pulls American Spirits from his jacket pocket. He lights his cigarette, leaves the pack on the coffee table.

"I think Silas is hot, right?" Delia turns to Nikki, who shrugs.

Nikki's inventorying Somerset's apartment: empty beers by the trash, a wad of dirty paper towels on the counter. He doesn't seem as put together as at the start of school. His eyes are sunken. The air is rank, like a boy's dorm room.

"You know who's really hot, though?" Nikki says.

Somerset laughs. "Nikki, are you capable of watching the show for any other reason than the guys?"

70

Jealous, the girls say with their eyes to each other.

"The uncle," Delia says.

"Superhot," Nikki says.

Somerset hits the bathroom. The second Delia hears the door close, she snags two smokes from his pack, stashes them in her shirt pocket.

"No way!" Nikki whispers happily. "He's going to know."

"Who cares? That's why he put them there."

Nikki's impressed. It's funny how Delia is brazen one minute, then shy with Greg. Somerset ambles back.

"Did you put the seat down, I hope?" Delia nags.

"I did," he says, feigning submissive obedience.

Later, when the girls walk home under bright constellations, they agree wholeheartedly: "He's in *love* with us!"

"It's out of control," Nikki says as they stop to light the stolen goods in the shadow of the tennis shack.

"Poor thing." Delia sighs, blowing smoke out of her worldly mouth.

Greg and Delia meet at the snack bar the next night. They sit with a big crowd, but the way they sit next to each other lets everyone know they're with each other. It's only at curfew, when the room starts shuffling around to leave, that Delia feels a chill. She can't tell where the draft is coming from—it could be that table of white girls over there, or the two black guys on the football team in line to grab food to go, who keep glancing back. She wonders for the first time if there's any other biracial couple at Wellington.

Back home, her group was mixed. And everyone talked about race; it was an easy conversation. It was part of how girls discussed guys. *Oh yeah, I love that kid Justin, you know who I mean? Yeah, he's half Mexican, right? Crazy blue eyes. You know that dude that just moved from Oakland? Anthony? Black guy, drives a black Mazda with the gold cross hanging from the rearview? That boy is superfine.*

Delia likes black boys. She likes white boys, but she likes black boys better. And she already knows that she can't say that out loud here. Black boys like her better than white boys do, too. She's bigger than skinny white girls, and stronger. White boys who grew up in black neighborhoods like her better than they like super-skinny white girls, but white boys who are truly white like the Olsen twins. *So what? What's wrong with being honest about it? We're all allowed to like what we like.* It's not that love comes down to skin or body—it has more to do with how someone moves, the aesthetics of sexuality in a group, the examples of love they saw growing up.

Her friend Jesse, who's a quarter black, a quarter white, and half Filipino, used to say that it's "culture not color." He belonged to a tribe innately savvy about race. "My stats is more Asian," he stated, lighting a cigarette. "But it's not

72

like I can be broke down into pieces. I'm made up of my experience."

Greg walks Delia to her dorm, kisses her under the Japanese maple. Its leaves shivering, red in the darkness. Greg rubs her hands between his own, warming her, and then lets her go.

"Goodnight, baby," he says over his shoulder.

"G'night," she manages to get out.

A shimmering afternoon in October brings a large crowd to boys' Varsity soccer. Parker, Nikki, and Delia sit on the sideline with parents and college scouts. The team has reinvented itself with a new starting lineup this year: three South Americans, including Gabriel, two Jamaicans, and one Italian kid.

The girls cheer every time Gabriel, the striker, boots the ball back upfield. Delia watches Nikki. "How *cute* is he?"

Nikki rolls her eyes. "Jesus, not again."

"What? I'm just saying he looks cute out there." Delia nudges Parker and they both smile.

"Ha-ha-ha. I hate you both." Nikki raises her eyebrows.

"Yo. Don't fucking look at me like that," Delia says in that half-kidding tone.

A parent looks down and the girls stifle laughter.

"You all having fun?" Gabriel trots to the sideline, holding the ball, his brow covered in sweat. He smiles at Nikki.

"What's up, Nicole?"

Gabriel turns and throws the ball into play. Nikki looks over at Parker and Delia. "Don't," she warns, and they dissolve into hysterics.

"What's up, Nicole?" Delia asks in a deep voice.

It seems this year, with the vise of academic pressure and less and less time to do anything, sexual tension is blooming on campus. The girls sprawl on the grass, bodies offered to the sun.

And Nikki *is* watching him. He moves better than anyone on the field, and he moves better here than he does in the halls. It's like learning a new song, this exercise in possibility and imagination: *Could I go out with him?*

Ever since Nikki was born, practically, she's been in love with someone. She has photographs of herself and Brian, her dad's best friend's son. They're one and a half, naked in a Pepto-Bismol pink tub, a rubber frog between them. The camera's flash turned their eyes red. Nikki's mother's hand, with its amethyst ring and gold bracelets, holds Nikki by the fat torso. Brian and Nikki are grinning. In middle school she made Neil eat glue, and gave Trent four Barbie valentines, and beat up Joseph on the bus. In junior high, she spent hours on the playground hanging from monkey bars, making dumb talk with boys in Avirex jackets and black jeans, steam rolling from their mouths.

How would Seth find out anyway? It's not like he has any

friends left here. He poured gasoline onto every bridge before he left, and then struck a match. And the school is like a maximum-security country club; they practically read all letters coming in or going out. The density of privilege alone is like a moat. Her life here is duct-taped shut.

"Hey, Cosby? Grab me a Coke," Chase calls to Greg in the snack bar line. It's Break, the half hour before Check In.

"You got it, White Bread."

Nikki tosses a fry in Chase's direction. "God, you're an asshole."

Chase and Greg are in a sociology class that's examining race and gender through twentieth-century popular culture, and although it should dispel some friction between them, it's exacerbated it instead. Greg sometimes acts like he truly doesn't like Chase. But then again, Chase is being unlikable this year. Some sweetness in him has turned sour.

Chase shrugs as if he did nothing wrong, and nods in Gabriel's direction. "What about you, Pelé? You score today?"

"I told you, I play defense."

"Weak."

"Oh, shut up, Chase, you don't play varsity anything," Nikki says. "Gabe was awesome."

"First of all, I play tennis. Second of all, I think we have a border-patrol love connection here. Anyone?" Chase looks around the table, but no one bites.

Nikki can feel Gabriel's leg almost resting against hers. She lets her knee fall gently against his. She can tell he's startled but is trying to keep his face composed.

Greg holds two chocolate chip cookies and hands one to Delia. "Here ya go, Deals."

"Where's *mine*, Theo?" Chase asks.

"Told you to quit that shit. Get it yourself, you redneck."

Chase slaps him on the head and slides out. "I'm gone anyway."

Greg slaps him back. Nikki stands.

"Are you leaving?" Gabriel asks, and she can tell he's nervous.

"Yeah, I think so. You want to walk?" Nikki sees Greg and Delia smirking.

"Um, sure." Gabriel's face is flushed.

"Okay, guys. See you later." Nikki grabs Gabriel's hand. They walk. The grass is white with frost, and they breathe out steam. Neither can think of anything to say. She leads Gabriel to the back entrance of Gray and smiles.

"Well, thanks for *escorting* me," she says, and they laugh.

"Sure, sure, anytime," he says, hands in pockets.

She kisses him on the cheek, leaving raspberry gloss. Then she turns to walk into the dormitory, and when she looks back, he's still standing there, his hands in his pockets, but grinning. Like the happy-go-lucky star of a black-and-white movie. She lets the door close.

When she gets upstairs, her heart is pounding. *What am I doing?*

She sits in a bathroom stall even though she doesn't have to pee. The sanitary bin is full, the lid pushed open. A sticker from the back of a maxi-pad on the floor. Nikki feels dirty, powerful. She puts her face in her hands, and her mouth feels hot. Then there's the other side of her rush: She can't wait to tell Delia.

7

Parker and Nikki slurp milk shakes in the snack bar Wednesday afternoon. They look on to the grounds from the window, at the breeze tossing the trees. Parker's nail polish is eggplant purple, and she has words written down each finger, like titles on the spines of books.

They've been talking about Nikki going out with Gabriel.

"I mean, it's whatever you want to do," Parker finally pronounces. "I think it's cool if Seth thinks it's cool."

Parker was the only one to know about Nikki's promise. Nikki called her from the San Diego airport the next day. And now she just lied to Parker and told her that she and Seth agreed to see other people, but not sleep with anyone else.

"I don't know," Nikki says, unable to meet Parker's eye.

"It's like, so far, all it's been is that kiss last week. On the cheek, nothing major. And afterwards I had butterflies."

Parker shrugs it off, smiles. "He's *beautiful*."

Nikki grins, her newsboy cap tilted over her eyes. When something is new, it makes her grin—part thrill, part shyness, part expectation, part reluctance. "Yeah, he is. That's the thing: I think he's beautiful and smart and cool. I just don't feel it."

"He's got like a little early Bob Dylan in him, and some *Y Tu Mamá También*, and a tiny bit of Orlando."

"You're out of your mind," Nikki says casually.

When Laine approaches, Nikki drags her high-heeled Steve Madden boots off the booth seat across from her and makes room. Laine sits with exaggerated fatigue. Her hair in a ponytail, white corduroy blazer, brown riding boots, tweed skirt.

She looks like a London schoolgirl, tired and in need of tea and crumpets, Nikki thinks.

Laine rests one cheek on her books, and moans. "Chemistry is going to kill me."

"Yeah, I'll be doing anything to avoid that one. There's just no way," Parker says.

The girl tribe is like drinks on a tray; you add another glass, and must restabilize your hold. Nikki could diagram it: her own defensiveness about being Laine's friend, even though Parker never overtly looks down on it. Parker's jealousy of Laine over Chase, Laine's guilt about Chase and also the Crash Test Bet, Parker's and Nikki's guilt for not having seen Laine's own crash coming. The fear each has that the other girls see them as slutty or prudish or inexperienced or over-experienced. The defenses and the bragging and the white lies about family and friends back home, about money or the lack of it, about crushes and lusts and disappointments.

And Delia, still on the outside of this diagram.

The bell clangs, and kids flood the halls. Delia swaggers up to the booth.

"What's up, sisters?"

She only technically meets the dress code in her blue-white-mulberry-plaid pants and her big sweater. She plunks down.

"What are you kids talking about?" she asks.

And the cocktails slide to the other side.

"Nothing much," Parker says.

Delia wonders if she's serious. Every time she sits with these girls, they talk about the Gold and Silver Ball, or Schuyler Covington, or the night they got written on, or Costa Rica. It's impossible to believe they aren't trying to alienate her—at least Laine and Parker. Hoarding their queen.

"How was hanging out with Greg last night?" Nikki asks.

"Good," she says shyly.

"How good?" Nikki asks.

"Not *that* good, sister, relax," she answers. "I'll tell you later."

Uh-oh, glasses crashing, Nikki thinks. Parker and Laine already feel left out of Nikki and Delia's friendship, and Delia, with a flourish of the knife, just cut them out entirely.

Delia makes hangdog eyes at the two. "You don't want to hear my sordid escapades, ladies."

Nikki turns her hat backward. "Not that sordid, from the sound of it."

Delia shrugs, reading a flyer above the napkin dispenser. "What's that?"

Laine takes it off the wall. "Apple picking. This Sunday."

"Hell." Nikki grins. "Who's the sponsor, the Bible club?"

"Naw, it's just a school trip," Parker says, reading the fine print.

"Let's go," Delia says.

"You're funny," Nikki says.

"Get out of this mental ward for a couple hours. Why not?"

"Why *not*?" Nikki asks. "Do you know what variety of supergeek is going to be on that bus, with their apple baskets all ready and their apple-picking outfits, like, washed and ironed?"

"I'll go," Parker says to Delia.

"Awesome," Delia says to Parker.

Glasses, sliding glasses, alert, alert.

"Are you going to go?" Nikki asks Laine.

"You have to!" Delia says.

Laine shrugs. "I guess," she says.

"I guess we're going apple picking," Nikki says darkly.

"It's a lot like pumpkin picking," Delia says, without fanfare, without even checking Nikki's reaction.

At Woods Crew, they sand the floor of a new cabin. Parker's talking to Jessica Irons, who has a crush on a new Upper-form named Kester Williamson. He's from Chicago, and is mysterious, plays drums, only hangs out with PGs. Nikki listens in, and feels her flannel shirt getting dank as she scours the floor.

"It's weird that he only hangs out with those older guys," Jessica says. "I don't get it."

Parker throws her braid behind her when it gets in her way. "Yeah, but all new Upper-forms are shady. Why would you leave your school after two years? When you have only two years left? Why would you want to make new friends?"

Nikki sits back on her heels, wipes sweat from her upper lip. "Who are you talking about?"

Parker and Jessica look at her. "Kester," Jessica says.

Nikki looks hard at Parker. The dust from their sanding hangs in the damp, woodsy air. Parker doesn't look away. "What?" she asks.

When Nikki gets too hot, she leaves her sandpaper square and walks down to the pond. The water is brackish, brown like black tea. The trees on the other shore are blotched with fiery color. Parker walks up behind her.

"Nik. When I was talking before about Kester, I was honestly talking about Kester. I like Delia. I didn't mean Delia."

"You think she's shady?"

Parker laughs in frustration. "No! Delia's not shady. She's cool. I just don't know her yet like you do."

Nikki throws a rock into the pond. It makes a deep *ploink*, sending up water around it. The ripples hurry from the center.

"Hey," Parker says. "So I talked to Chase this morning."

Nikki turns. "Are you serious?"

Parker nods. "I told him he was an asshole. He told me I was an asshole too."

Nikki stares. "Really?"

Parker nods. Nikki doesn't know what to say, so they keep watching each other's faces, and suddenly both start laughing. They laugh so hard they fall over, clumsily losing footing on the stony ground. Nikki throws her arm around her roommate. "Oh, babe," she says and sighs when she catches her breath.

Saturday night rolls around. The movie is *Fast Times at Ridgemont High*, and Nikki meets Gabriel at the doors to go inside. He's dressed in a pressed white shirt, ironed jeans, a sterling silver buckle, and Creed cologne. He's chewing Orbit and he keeps taking his hands out of his pockets as if he could hear some grandmother nagging him.

They sit in the dark auditorium like a 1950s couple with a chaperone behind them. Gabriel is so still Nikki thinks he's afraid to breathe. When they go to the snack bar, he buys her a soda and a cookie, and Nikki feels the room's derision. She juts out her chin. *Christ, I'm with the mama's boy.*

She refuses to go anywhere, not that he asks or even makes her feel as though she should, so they wait out Saturday night in the snack bar, sitting across a table from each other. They joke and Nikki frequently crosses the line from playful to cruel. She points out that she always thinks he has something on his face, but it's just his mole. When he stumbles over idioms, she mimics his accent.

"It's all the way you play the game," he says at one point.

And she rears back in her chair, imitating his posture, and invokes Pablo Escobar: "'It's all *in* the way you play the game.'"

And he takes it, smiling down at his hands.

The whole night, she scans the halls beyond the room for Delia or Greg.

When Check In nears, she lets him walk her back. The nearer they get to Gray and to the end of the evening, the worse she feels. She's been a bitch from start to finish.

They stand under the Japanese maple, whose leaves are translucent red. Nikki, out of a need for redemption, takes his hands. She swings his arms, looks him in the eye.

"Goodnight, Gabriel," she says, drawing out the words so that it's provocative.

"Goodnight," he says.

She kisses him, long and lusciously and honestly. Touches his cheek with her finger. Lets her hand brush his chest as it falls. He takes a deep breath. She's delivered sweet dreams after all.

Greg and Delia skip the movie and the dance, to have the choir loft to themselves. They fool around for hours, elevated above the pews and the altar, hidden. They take breaks, lie in each other's arms on the floor, and tell stories. Delia likes this pattern; kissing, playing, then hearing about his childhood, the guys back home in Brooklyn, the good guys and the bad guys, his sister, the trouble she makes, how his parents deal with it. What Greg did wrong as a kid. His adventures and misadventures. Visiting his grandparents in the West Indies, his first girlfriend in second grade (a Puerto Rican girl named Lisa Juarez), his favorite food.

"I feel like the FBI is investigating me or some shit," he whispers.

"Well, ask me a goddamn question, you retard, I'm

doing all the asking just because."

"You are *mean*, Delia."

"You like it and you know it."

"I do kind of like you, but not really," he deadpans.

"Oh, shut up," she says, pulling out of his arms to smack his wide chest.

"I do kind of like you," he says again, but in a different, simple tone.

And she swoons.

The next morning Delia lazily looks at the clock, then sits upright. They're going apple picking.

Nikki kicks the door open like a gangster. "Git the eff up, sleeping beauty, this was your idea."

Delia straggles out of her sheets, pulls on Levi's, throws on a surf sweatshirt and cowboy boots. "Let's do it," she croaks.

"How come you didn't come to the movie or anything?" Nikki asks evenly.

"We skipped it all," Delia says jubilantly. "We just hung out all night together."

Nikki tries to laugh good-naturedly. "Well, that's good for you, but sad for me and my dear friend Gabe, who were expecting to see you."

"Oh my God, are you mad?"

"No, I'm not *mad*." Nikki lies. "I just thought it was

going to be fun. I thought it was the point."

"Oh my God," Delia says again. "It *is* the point. Let's do something fun this week, the four of us. Dude, I'm so sorry."

"Chill." Nikki laughs.

They meet Parker and Laine at the Wellington van. About ten other kids are getting in, mostly Preps with nothing better to do.

As they drive, Parker sketches apples on her jeans with a felt-tip pen. Laine presses her forehead against the glass, and Delia and Nikki push each other, like ten-year-olds on a road trip. All Delia wants today is to feel part of this crew. She misses her girlfriends from back home; she missed them for a number of reasons before she even left California.

After passing through Glendon, then the strip malls, and then some trailer-park no-man's-land, the van makes an arc onto a dirt drive. A wooden sign: FREEMAN'S ORCHARD, U PICK IT. CIDER. PIE. APPLEJACK.

"Mmmh, I could use some applejack," Parker muses.

"What *is* applejack?" Nikki asks.

"I'm not sure, but it sounds delicious, and I bet I'm not allowed to have it, so I want it."

The girls stand to get off the van. Nikki turns her Yankees baseball hat backward, pops her gum, mutters something about manual labor on a Sunday. They all jump out onto gold grass.

"Put us to work," Nikki says to no one, as if they were migrant pickers.

A man in suspenders with few teeth left in his mouth gives them garbled directions, and points to a stack of baskets near the shop. The girls each fetch one and spread out separately into the orchard. Delia thought they would wander together, but she finds herself alone and feels like a leper.

Nothing to do but walk then. Delia's been to orange and lemon groves, where fruit melts in the California sunshine, but this is different. The cold blue sky is what makes an apple good. It's a different means of nurturing.

She feels high after waking up lethargic. The sun glitters from apple cheeks like gold stars. She moves down a row, past limbs with black knots for knuckles. The skin, she sees as she twists apples from their branches, is occasionally pocked by a bird or scarred by weather, but when she takes a crunch, the flesh is snow-white.

Delia sits down in the grass.

The girls are spread through the orchard, their jackets dappled, hair shining. These girls are *weird*. In her hometown, she knew every friend's family, house, and bedroom. These girls have no context. They exist, floating without the gravity of history, in Wellington. As if they were born in the delivery room of the school, and pulled with forceps from their dorms.

Nikki, with her white North Face jacket and black Versace glasses, throwing an apple into the air and catching it. Parker, in a long red coat and gold sneakers, staring now into a tree. And Laine, where did she go? The lost girl, who finds herself every few hours or days, who is included and excluded, by the others, by herself.

This is Delia's family now. This is who she lives with, for Christ's sake.

The shadow of a tree falls across her blue jeans. She goes over reasons, like a grocery list, for why the girls might not like her. But the sky is too beautiful. She doesn't have the heart. Once in a while, she finds the power—the one her mother begs her to use—to be herself. She languishes there and collects her confidence, decides to forget what anyone else thinks. So simple and *so* difficult. It's the only option and the only solution.

Someone rings a cowbell, and the group congregates for hot cider and just-baked apple turnovers, their seams crimped and glued with hardening apple syrup. When the girls bite into them, steam comes out, and they wave at their mouths to cool them off. Delia asks who got the most apples and walks around the group; a small kid named Addison, whose red hair is combed over like it's school picture day, has the most bountiful basket.

They have another hour. Some kids go to look at the chickens laying eggs in the shed, and Parker beckons to her group. They follow her down a row to the end and across a ravine. In the shady woods on the other side is the stone foundation of what once was a house. The girls perch on the inside, sipping their warm ciders. The silence is deep, cold, dank. Parker rolls a cigarette, and Delia bumps a smoke out of her Camel Lights pack. Offers one to Nikki.

"No thanks," Nikki says.

Parker lights her own. "You want a hand-roll?"

"No," Nikki says. "I don't smoke anymore."

"Say that again?" Parker says, flicking her match flame out and dropping it.

Nikki shrugs, looks around evasively, shoulders hunched.

"You quit?" asks Laine.

"Yeah. You know, my mom died of lung cancer. She smoked like three packs of Kools a day. So."

Both Delia and Parker freeze mid-drag. Nikki's never talked openly about the actual sickness. Delia puts out her cigarette on the pine-needle floor.

"I quit, too," Delia says.

Nikki laughs, embarrassed. "Come on, don't be stupid."

"I'm completely serious," Delia says.

Parker is exhaling, the cigarette between her long fingers, and looking at Nikki with big brown eyes. She's thinking.

"I command you to finish that butt, Park."

"Don't tell me what to do," Parker says.

"I will kill you if you stop smoking," Nikki says, laughing, giddy and foolish to be the center of things.

Laine is rubbing her fingers on lichen, watching.

"This is like giving up food and water put together," Parker says, crushing her half-smoked butt under her sneaker.

"No, fuck you!" Nikki laughs. "Light another one."

"Sorry." Parker smiles, albeit wistfully. "Besides, who knows if this will last. I'm going to try. If I start seeing things and getting the shakes, hopefully American Spirits will take me back in, even after I betrayed them like this."

The girls stand there in this stone structure, feeling at ease. Except for Laine, obviously, because she clears her throat.

"I'd love to give it up, Nik," she says very seriously. "But I don't smoke."

This breaks everyone else into laughter, and Nikki throws an arm around Laine's shoulders. She swings Laine's stoic body, their shoes scuffing up the dead leaves, and Laine eventually laughs too. Parker catches Delia's eye and winks. If Delia steps up to the afternoon, maybe the afternoon can make good on it.

8

Delia waits at Greg's dorm entrance. The afternoon got cold the second the magenta sun dipped under the horizon, and she rubs her arms. When a kid walks up, she hands him the apple.

"Don't ask," she says.

The kid, a Prep from Iran and barely five feet, looks at her fearfully. "For me?"

"No," she says, laughing. "Can you give it to Greg, on the third floor? Tell him it's from Delia. Don't eat it!"

"Okay," the guy says, cowed, taking her seriously.

"Thanks, dude."

Walking to Gray, she tries to feel sweet and innocuous. All she wanted was to leave him an apple, right? What could be simpler? But her eyes are sad and her mouth is worried.

She's been here before. The need to see a guy too often, the desire to touch him, check on him, and know what he's doing.

The foursome has a double-date, dinner at the Chinese restaurant in Glendon. It's Delia's idea, to make up for how much time she spends alone with Greg. She can tell Nikki's pissed lately. The excursion would probably be more fun but Greg is running late from football, and when they arrive, the restaurant is kind of shutting down. Gabriel, because he always orders for Nikki, dictates ten plates of food for the crew.

The waitress, in a dress embroidered with blossoms and butterflies, nods and pours tea. The group tries to relax, talks about how starving they are, throws balled-up chopstick wrappers at one another. But strangely, they have nothing much to say tonight. Gabriel seems especially self-conscious, as though he doesn't know the procedure for this exact dynamic. The food comes in stages, plate by steaming plate. They get busy eating.

"Yo, I'm about to tear this shit apart," Greg says, his fork hovering above the fried rice like a predator. Greg isn't here to make conversation; he's famished.

They chow down, and share everything, and barely finish half of what they ordered. Greg asks for it all to be boxed up, though, because his appetite will return in an hour. They get the bill on a tray with fortune cookies. Gabriel looks to Greg.

"Half and half?"

Greg looks at the money in his billfold, and Delia realizes he hasn't got enough to cover her. But she doesn't want to embarrass him by offering cash. Gabriel finally gets the problem after Greg paws through his wallet for another minute.

"Wait," Gabriel says. "Can you get the next one? I'll get this one."

"Yeah, sure," Greg says in a voice meant to sound cavalier.

Greg says he'll pay for the cab back, but when they get to school, he lets everyone step out besides Delia. "Hey, babe, do you have two dollars?" he asks quietly.

"Of course," she says, and gives him a five.

Nikki belches into the wind.

"Oh my God, you are gross!" Delia laughs.

The girls walk to the dorm, rubbing their stomachs.

"So that was fun, right?" Nikki asks unsurely.

"Yeah," Delia forces herself to agree.

September vanishes, day by day, and the trees turn postcard colors, and the town swells with tourists who drive through and stop to eat lunch. In tortoiseshell glasses, driving old Cadillacs, these emissaries from the outside world watch the Wellington students as if they were local wildlife, too. Nikki likes smelling the first wood smoke of this autumn: She has come this way before.

Although the way the light dissipates earlier, and the evening hurries to catch you—this strikes a chord in Nikki, a foreboding.

Today at Woods Crew, they're tying burlap sacks over saplings' heads. She and Parker are getting along. Lately, it's been touch and go. It's not like they fight. It's just that sometimes, Nikki feels the chill of being evaluated by Parker. Like when Parker asks about Seth or Gabriel, she seems to be asking Nikki if she's being honest.

But today the crew is packed into the windowless Suburban, with shovels and twine and pruning shears. The truck rocks, and they sing to "Every Rose Has Its Thorn" at the tops of their voices.

"Every cowboy sings his sad, sad song . . ."

Grant, the progressive-minded, New Zealand astronomy teacher who leads Woods Crew, drives the rutted road through the woods, his fingerless gloves on the wheel, and smiles at the gang's off-pitch effort.

Afterward, Parker and Nikki talk loudly, stall to stall, over their own showers, rubbing mud off their hands in hot water.

In the room, Parker has stockpiled art materials. "I have to create a castle made of sand. Can you believe that?"

"Actually, yes," Nikki says, believing anything about Parker's endeavors and understanding none of them. "What's the assignment?"

"To turn a song, the words or music, into something tangible."

"Sometimes I get confused. I'm freaking memorizing algebra formulas and you're pasting sand onto a turret. Are we at the same school?"

"You could help me if you weren't going to the movies."

"Naw," Nikki says lazily, pulling on socks and boots. "Me and Deals promised."

Parker looks up from the floor, where she's sitting in a huge hoodie and black silk pajama pants. "Really?"

"Yeah."

"And you really think it's kosher?"

"Why wouldn't it be? He's our advisor." Nikki thrusts her arms into her jacket, annoyed at what she feels is jealousy on Parker's part. "I'll see you later."

"Hey, Nik, I didn't mean anything."

Nikki pauses by the door, and smiles. "I know." But as she walks down the stairs, she mutters, "Annoying! Jesus."

"Whassup?" Delia grins when she opens her door. She's got on jeans, a hoodie, a flannel jacket over it, and her long hair is combed for once. "Let's do it," Delia says.

They saunter in the dark, hands wedged deep in their pockets, to Somerset's house. The sky is punctuated with stars. Already, both of them are giddy, having been invited off grounds.

"Ever notice that when we see him, he doesn't know how to greet us? He almost goes to kiss us, like we're family arriving at Thanksgiving or some shit? Do you know what I'm saying?" Delia asks.

"Completely. Yeah. He gets all awkward with his hands."

The girls approach his house, windows orange with light. They rake their hair and straighten their jackets after they knock.

"Hello hello," he says, as he often says. His dirty-blond hair swept up in its messy way.

"Hello hello," Delia mimics, and the girls giggle.

Somerset rolls his eyes, smiling. "Oh, for Christ's sake, get in the car."

Delia takes shotgun, and messes with the radio till Somerset tells her to put something on and leave it, she's driving him crazy. He likes to act fed up with them. Delia starts going through his glove compartment.

"What are you doing?" he asks with emphasized annoyance.

"Don't you have a pipe in here or something, dude? I mean, come on, we're going to the movies."

"I hope you're kidding," he says.

Delia slams the glove compartment door, sits back, blows air out the side of her mouth.

He looks at her. She grins. He looks away, then looks at his rearview, his eyes almost worried.

"Why are you no fun tonight, Patrick?" Delia kids.

"I'm fun, I'm fun," Somerset says distractedly as he slows for a red light.

"Any good teacher gossip?" Delia asks.

"Yeah, what's happening in the old teachers' lounge?" Nikki adds.

Somerset shrugs. "If only you could know how little goes on. Just try to imagine a bunch of adults, sequestered in a nowhere town that's cold ten months of the year." He looks at the girls with chagrin. "Sorry, I'm a bit surly this evening. But no more! We're here."

When they get out of the car, the parking lot looks like a place from the end of the world. Broken glass glitters at its edges, dead grass grows over the curbs, Queen Anne's Lace shivers against the black tar, and only three other cars are parked here. Their shoes crunch the grit of the pavement.

"Beautiful area, meant to tell you guys that," Delia deadpans as if Nikki and Somerset are her hosts in the northeast, which they kind of are.

Inside, they get popcorn, soda, and candy. Somerset lets them buy their own tickets but treats them to everything else. This seems to be the proper breakdown. Any more and it would seem like a date.

Later, when they drive back to school on the empty roads, Nikki sits shotgun, and they chat about the film, making fun of Delia because she cried.

"You're a pussy," Nikki says.

"Did you hear what she said!" Delia screeches as if she was a choirgirl.

Nikki steals glances at Somerset's big hands on the wheel. Whatever sadness had plagued him before they went into the theater has dissolved, and he's back to being jovial. She gets misty now, because perhaps this venture *hadn't*, in fact, seemed kosher. Perhaps she'd had her own misgivings, which is why she'd wanted to backhand Parker on her way out.

But here they are, going just under the speed limit past ghostly power stations and empty mechanic shops, whose windows are darker than the night, and she's cozy, the heat roaring, with two friends. In this mixed-up, rules-crazy Wellington world, she's riding with comrades.

9

Nikki and Gabriel have developed a formal relationship; they walk each other to classes and back to their dorms, talk a lot, kiss goodnight, and are considered a couple. But they never hook up; Nikki's bossy and controlling enough to prevent them from ever getting to an isolated spot, and Gabriel is too polite and shy to push.

They have one special spot: a marble bench built into the wall near the chapel foyer. The domed ceiling is painted with angels, reaching chubby arms at doves. A chandelier slowly spins in the breeze, and the shadows rotate.

"Tell me more," Nikki says.

"Let's see," he says, racking his childhood for another story.

Because to her, he's a star. Almost a prince, although

technically just the son of a politician. He's an heir. He's a paparazzi picture in *OK!* He's one of Wellington's celebrities.

Her favorite story so far is from when he was only four. Too young to understand the emergency until a bodyguard swept into his and his sister's room, snatched them from their lacy beds, and took them through back hallways never used, to an underground armored van never driven. They were screeching down the drive as Gabriel looked out the window, and saw one of the guard dogs—Chi-chi—lying by the iron gate, a dark splotch leaking from his ear.

Tonight he tells her about a ball his family attended in Barcelona. Nikki plays with his cuffs as he talks, turning his cuff links. They served twelve courses at a long, gold table, including a pig that had been roasting for days. And afterward, everyone danced to an orchestra.

"You danced, like, you know, a waltz?" she asks.

"Yeah," he says. "I'll show you."

"No!" Nikki squeals.

"Come on, get up," he says as he stands.

She lets him lead, but she can't stop laughing. It somehow feels strange to be so close to him, she can't get used to it. They turn a few times, in the dusky room, and then she finally pushes him away.

"I can't do it!" she says, and sits down, still giggling.

* * *

Gabriel, Greg, and Laine all have away games Saturday, so Parker and Nikki wander to Delia's game. It's warm, in the seventies, for early October. What once was to be enjoyed, a stolen summer day that lands in fall, is now a sign of the apocalypse. Everywhere people talk about global warming, shaking their heads severely, clucking their tongues in this learned eco-melancholy.

Parker's swinging her bare arms. She's wearing a wifebeater and black jeans, her Adidas sneakers. Earlier in the day, she let a new Lower-form named Joel write on her forearm, in the same format as ingredients listed on food packages. Except he listed *soul (1 mg); freakiness (100% RDA)*, etc.

"How truly retarded," Nikki says casually.

Parker sneezes. "Jesus! It's that goldenrod," she says, pointing out the late-blooming yellow ragweed at the edge of the woods. "I don't know, I think it's funny."

"You like Joel?"

Parker shrugs. "He's smart. And kind of anarchic. And he grew up in Montana with four llamas as pets."

"You so didn't answer the question."

Parker smiles. "I know."

Nikki hopes they don't run into Chase today. Walking around campus with Parker makes her nervous because he can pop up anywhere, like a video game killer hoisting his gun suddenly over a digital hedge or saloon door. And then Parker will go into an hour of muddy-eyed silence. Nikki's tried to get her out of these moods, but Parker puts her long fingers on her chin, thinking without communicating, brooding without pitying herself, looking without seeing.

They crest the hill above the girls' playing fields. Girls heave red-faced on the field, and players who were just substituted out squirt water into their mouths when they have the strength to raise their arms. Black smudges on cheekbones absorb light. The referee trots with the play down the field, the whistle permanently between his lips.

They plop down in the grass, far from anyone else. Parker lies back, in a crucifixion pose.

"That feels nice," she says, basking in the sun.

"Yee-ha! Go Deals! Go Deals!" Nikki shouts.

"You have to be my Howard Cosell," Parker says, eyes closed luxuriously.

"Well, let's see." Nikki looks at Parker. She can never tell if Parker is being snide about Delia, or if the two just haven't connected. It's the same problem everyone has with Parker; she's outside everything to some extent. Although not with Nikki.

So Nikki narrates the play. A Deerfield redhead takes it halfway to the goal but a Wellington girl turns it around, passes to Delia, who's streaking to the Deerfield goal.

"Oh boy," Nikki says. "Delia's got it, she's going to the goal, oh wow. She's close."

"Shoot!" Parker coaches lazily from her reclining state.

"Oh my God, she just kicked it! But a girl stopped her, stopped the ball. Wait a minute." A whistle blows.

"What's up?"

"They look like they're screaming at each other." Delia's now pointing a finger at the other girl, aggressively moving toward her. "Holy shit," Nikki says.

Parker pulls herself up, dazed. Holds hand above her eyes to see. "Whoa. She's going crazy."

The referee is holding Delia back. Delia stomps away, and no card is given to either player. The game resumes. Parker and Nikki are quiet, watching more intently. There's tricky snatches of the ball by an adept toe, and the energy surges like the tide. But suddenly Delia and the same Deerfield girl are racing alone, Delia sweating to catch up because the girl somehow has the field to herself if Delia doesn't reach her. The goalie is dancing, trying to ready herself, flexing gloved fingers in the sunshine.

And then Delia does something amazing. She lunges forward and her foot neatly catches the girl's back foot, and they both go down, so hard they raise dust, and their bodies bounce.

"Holy shit," Nikki says.

"Wow," Parker says.

They're both impressed and disturbed.

"She's like Mike Tyson, biting ears off and shit," Nikki says.

The coaches lumber fast onto the field, hackles raised, and assistant coaches scamper to keep up. Parker looks at Nikki. "Do you want to like, maybe—"

"Um, do absolutely anything else but watch the rest of this game?"

"Yeah."

They walk up the sunny incline, laughing. Looking back occasionally.

"She went bananas, dude," Nikki keeps saying.

Later, in the dorm, Nikki hears about how Delia wouldn't shake the hands of the opposing team when both teams lined up to do so. She kept her hands firmly down at her sides, looked straight ahead. She got a verbal thrashing from the coach, since sportsmanship is placed above all else at Wellington.

At the snack bar that night, Gabriel and Greg and Delia and Nikki are sitting in a booth, sharing fries. They've been avoiding the subject of Delia's game, but Nikki feels compelled to bring it up. "Hey, Deals. Did you see me and Park out there today?"

Delia slaps a fry into her mouth, eyes narrowing at Nikki. "No," she lies.

"You went totally psycho!"

Delia's eyes are tiny slits. "Gee, thanks." *Why are you doing this?*

The guys look at each other nervously, aware they're in the range of violent girl emotions.

"I don't mean anything. It was kind of cool," Nikki says, which is almost true. *Why am I doing this?*

"Well," Delia says in a shaky voice, "that girl was from California. I knew her."

Nikki nods, making her *and-so?* face.

"She said things to me."

"What did she say?" Nikki scoffs.

Delia gives her one last, long look. "I think I'm heading back. Greg, come on." She shoves Greg out of the booth.

"Whoa, girl!" Greg says, laughing in a low voice. "We're going, we're going."

"What are you *doing*?" Nikki spits out as if Delia is acting crazy again.

"Whatever, Nik," Delia mutters as they leave, her arm hooked through Greg's.

Nikki sips her Diet Coke and feels Gabriel look at her and look away. She knows he's too polite to pursue this. Greg is probably talking Delia off the edge of the cliff, but Gabriel can't do that for Nikki. So they sit in awkward silence until curfew. She kisses him on the lips outside the student center and suggests they both head home, there's no need for him to walk her.

Later, Delia sits at her desk, staring at her hand. Her birthmark is the red of a summer tomato. People sometimes point it out to her, as if it was paint. She catches them wincing when they realize it's not.

But for her, it is what it is. Her eyes are brown and always have been. Her name is Delia and always will be. And her hand is marked. It doesn't mean anything. It doesn't mean nothing.

But lately she's been wondering why it's there. A person can always know they're on some threshold when they question the tenets of his or her self.

The next day is Nikki's birthday, and when she wakes up, she tries to push the skirmish with Delia out of her head.

Nicole Olivetti is seventeen today.

Last year, she barely knew anyone (including herself) at this point in the school year. The floormaster threw her a feed after study hall. The kitchen staff provided an enormous, sugary, grossly creamy cake, with raspberry filling. The girls gorged. Nikki alone ate two lavender icing flowers and lay all night in bed with a bellyache and anxiety about being sixteen. Sixteen was an age to accomplish huge things: true love and blossoming into beauty and becoming super popular.

Girls at home got BMWs and parties at catering halls with Sean Paul tribute bands. They wore brand-new Manolos—soles un-scuffed—and someone brought cocaine in an exotic red vial from the city. Everyone treated the birthday girl, whoever it was, like a princess that night. That was the rule. And here, Nikki got a nasty cake sitting on a carpet with a bunch of near-strangers.

But this year might be different. Seventeen is serious. It's low profile and elegant. Not so bloated with celebration and ritual. *It feels real,* she thinks, getting up in her pajamas this morning to look at a world bathed in a tender, misty light. It must have rained in the night, because the air feels fresh and wet even though the sun is slowly drying it out. She opens the window and leans on the sill to breathe in the air of her birthday morning, and birds make a chaotic song.

"Happy birthday, Nik," Parker croaks from her bed.

They hit the dining hall and eat brunch. Nikki didn't pick up Delia from her room on the way, as is their habit, and Delia doesn't show up either. Amy Brant decorates a bagel with cream cheese and raisins to make a cupcake, and Nikki slouches in her seat, pulls her Yankees cap down farther, as they present it and sing happy birthday.

"That is so disgusting," she mutters as they sing, and they laugh, because it is.

She and Parker head out of the dining hall, and the anxiety about Delia only increases. The small wound hangs open, unbandaged, unstitched. It's just a little cut, but it feels wrong, even if it doesn't exactly hurt.

But here she is, coming into the dining hall through the old glass-paned wood doors.

"I'll meet you back?" Parker asks, and leaves.

"What's up?" Nikki asks sullenly.

Delia's got her hands tucked into her sweatshirt's front pocket. "Can we go somewhere and talk?"

Nikki shrugs, not liking the sound of this.

"Do you mind if we go out to the cabin, to Kingston maybe, just to get out of here for a bit?"

Nikki shrugs again, morosely. As they exit the building, she starts to say that the whole thing is a misunderstanding.

"Can we wait till we get there?" Delia asks in a small voice.

So they proceed on the most awkward walk of Nikki's life. Past the art and dance buildings at the periphery of the grounds, through Happer Woods, picking over branches that came down in the rain and block the path. Deeper and deeper. Delia leading the way, holding blackberry branches, thin and prickly, for Nikki to take as she approaches.

"Careful," Delia says dolefully, her face straight and formal.

Screw you! Nikki can't help but think. *You know it's my birthday. What happened yesterday was not a big deal, and you're making it into a bigger deal. And for fuck's sake you started it! You were the psycho freak on the field!* Nikki is literally biting her tongue this time.

Kingston, in its damp and lichen-covered glory, appears.

"Here we are," Delia says in a weird voice, and Nikki's heart sinks further.

Delia bends to tie a lace that came undone, and Nikki pushes in the door, aggressively.

"*Surprise!*" the boys shout.

The cabin, so dark on the outside, is golden with candles on the inside. Gabriel and Greg are pointing and laughing at Nikki, whose jaw is dropped and heart is drag racing all over her rib cage.

"Oh my God," she manages.

Delia comes in, grinning ear to ear. There's a chocolate cake on the shelf, and scraggly wildflowers, late-blooming weeds really, in a few soda cans. Gabe is looking at Nikki, kind of mooning, but she doesn't mind right now.

"Oh my *God*," Nikki says again louder, and starts laughing.

"Ha-ha, I think we actually got you," Delia says, beaming.

"You totally did," Nikki says, hand still to her chest. "You guys . . ."

Greg hands her a purple Vitaminwater. "Special treat. Belvedere and purple water."

Nikki swigs and grimaces, wipes her lips. "You guys," she says again, shaking her head.

As Gabriel tunes the radio to a Rolling Stones song that almost comes through clear, Delia presents Nikki with a brown package with stamps on it. "From my mom," Delia says.

"Are you serious?" Nikki says.

Delia nods. Nikki slices the tape with a nail, careful not to hurt her French manicure, and pulls a smaller box from the tissue. Inside is a brown bracelet, tied on red string.

"They're seeds from this tree we have in California. A guy my mom knows, this old surfer dude, makes them and sells them on the beach. Anyway, she says it's a charm, and it means you'll have to come back to La Jolla soon."

Nikki asks Delia to clasp it onto her wrist.

"There you go," Delia says, and affectionately grabs Nikki's fingers to make the beads shake.

Nikki looks at her friend with wet eyes.

Delia makes a scoffing face. "You didn't think I was really pissed, did you? I would never get pissed at you, really, Nik."

Nikki hugs her tight.

"You're beautiful," Delia whispers. "Happy birthday, Nicole."

Over Delia's shoulder, Nikki sees the lyrics Seth spray-painted on the wall last year: COME IN, SHE SAID, I'LL GIVE YOU SHELTER FROM THE STORM. And now she's crying like a baby, soaking Delia's sweatshirt, and laughing at the same time.

"No crying on your birthday!" Delia says as the boys look on, partly alarmed, partly confused.

Nikki pulls away, runs her finger under each eye to wipe away mascara. "I love you guys," she says with a thick voice, and everyone starts laughing, including Nikki.

* * *

Gabriel asks Nikki where she wants to have her birthday dinner. For some reason she chooses the diner, even though he's ready to take her to the nicest restaurant in a fifty-mile radius. She's craving a grilled Reuben, with thousand island dressing, and crispy onion rings. And lemon meringue pie afterward. They sit at a chrome-bordered table. Gabriel hangs her coat and his own on the racks. She watches him scan the menu.

He is a good soul, I know he is. I know he is.

"She'll have the grilled Reuben," Gabriel tells the waitress. "And onion rings, extra crispy, please. I'll have a cheeseburger with fries. Two chocolate shakes."

When the waitress leaves, her ears glittering with cheap studs, Gabe reaches into his black overcoat on the rack for a red box. "Happy birthday, Nicole."

Nikki takes a breath and looks at the box, emblazoned with M&R. She hadn't expected this. She slowly opens it to find a necklace, two trinkets dangling on a gold chain.

"It's gorgeous," she says.

"I'm glad you like it." Gabriel smiles like a benefactor.

"Are you kidding? I love it."

"My sister got it in New York for me, from Me&Ro. It's her favorite spot."

Wow. Julia Velez picked this out. Nikki's enchanted by his sister, who ends up on Page Six and in *W*'s party pages, holding hands with Zac Posen and Marguerite Missoni and Keira Knightley.

"Is that a sapphire?" Nikki points to the blue stone dangling next to the gold leaf.

"Yes, it's your birthstone. And see, this ginkgo leaf, it's a good-luck charm."

This was the nicest gift any boyfriend had ever given Nikki. Seth gave her an iTunes playlist last year, and one of her Long Island boyfriends had given her a Jeremy Shockey jersey.

"Can I put it on you?" Gabriel asks.

"Sure." Nikki turns her head, allowing Gabriel to latch on the necklace.

The gold feels cool on her skin.

"You look beautiful," he says.

Nikki smiles. She feels like a princess, with this charm dropping into the cleavage of her white cashmere V-neck, slurping her shake. She's very happy all of a sudden, looking at Gabriel, who's unfolding his paper napkin. "Thank you, Gabe," she says.

He looks at her. He must realize she means it, because his smile is relieved.

It's over coffee and pie, which they share, that Gabriel slips. Nikki says she better get back, she feels bad for not spending more time with Delia, after she threw her a party today.

"I don't know," Nikki says, flipping the spoon of lemon gel over in her mouth. "I made her feel bad about her freakout on the field. I shouldn't have done that."

"That girl, the one who was taunting her, she was from her hometown, right?"

"Yeah," Nikki says, waiting for more.

"So that must have sucked."

Nikki stares, trying to figure him out. "Why?"

"You know. She was probably heckling her for why she left La Jolla."

"What do you mean?" Nikki says.

Gabriel stops stirring his coffee. "You know the rumors."

"Do I?"

"Don't you?"

"No," she says slowly.

He shrugs now, backtracking. "I mean, I don't know what's true and what's just a story."

"So tell me the stories."

Gabriel is now truly uncomfortable, looks away as he rips the top off the creamer. "I don't know. There's one about her and four guys from the football team." Gabriel checks her face for any recognition. "Or I also heard there was a video thing with this guy and this girl."

Nikki stares at him.

"Never mind," Gabriel says. "These are stories. I thought you'd heard them."

In the taxi back to school, driving through the night-time town, Gabriel leans in for a kiss, but Nikki turns away. She knows she should treat him better. Finally, Nikki kisses him long and hard. She feels the same aversion she had as a kid when she tried to eat yogurt or oatmeal.

Gabriel leans in to her body. His hands go over the contours of Nikki's cashmere sweater. She squirms.

Gabriel is oblivious to Nikki's response. One hand rubs the outside of her bra like he's putting on suntan lotion; Nikki gives Gabe more than a slight nudge.

He grunts and sits back, defeated and confused. "I'm sorry. I didn't know I was pushing."

"Just, you know, not in the cab," Nikki says quietly. "I think we should just wait, that's all."

"Okay, okay. God, I'm sorry."

But when they get back to campus, even though they have an hour before Check In, Nikki sweetly makes the excuse that she has so much homework. She practically runs from the parking lot where Gabriel is paying the driver in the lamplight. She walks fast across the grounds, the arched windows of the library lit up like a church. Her hands smell like fried food, and she can't wait to wash them.

In bed that night, as Parker snaps off the light, Nikki thinks and thinks. Finally, she asks her.

"Yeah, I heard them," Parker says. "I don't know if I believe any of them. They sound pretty much like bad after-school specials."

Nikki turns over in her blankets. The dorm is settling, like an enormous machine that's just been turned off but is still hot. "Why didn't you tell me?"

Parker's silent. "I don't know. If she wants you to know something, as her friend, she'll tell you. It's not my place."

Nikki tries to sleep, tries to clear her mind of these visions where wild and beautiful Delia gets blindsided. But it's like when she was little watching horror movies at friends' houses; she always clapped her hands over her eyes a millisecond too late.

10

The school has sunk into October, like a stone thrown into a lake. The students descend with beautiful gravity. When Nikki left the dorm, books in her faux Louis Vuitton backpack, eyeliner drawn on eyes too bleary to see themselves in the mirror, North Face unbuttoned to the morning sun, she could feel the gold charm on her sternum warming.

Now she's in Poli Sci, having finished a quiz on the origins of the modern Middle East conflict. Or, rather, almost finished. She has one question left, and she can't retrieve the answer from memory. Next to her, Balmain Trestin is sweating it out, scratching his zits and checking his TAG Heuer. Outside, a steeple points to heaven, disembodied from its church; all Nikki can see is a blaze of trees and the spire.

"Five more minutes, guys," Ms. Westerhouse says.

Shit. What's the answer? Nikki twirls her pencil. Balmain rubs his forehead and groans. For him, school is almost sexual, and it disgusts Nikki. He's so tied into the winning and losing, into perfection, it's taken the place of a girl in his life.

And there, across from Nikki, legs crossed, lustrous curls like a 1950s ad for shampoo, big hands resting over his quiz, is Gabriel. *The angel Gabriel.* He's even got a body like the angels in Renaissance paintings they studied in art history class—virile and innocent. He's looking at the floor, but he wants to look at her.

"One more minute, crew, and hand 'em in."

She often thinks of him as Romeo, in her head. Because his face seems doomed, and his eyes are very looking-up-at-her-on-the-balcony-while-I-outstretch-my-hand-and-make-a-formal-speech. *Why can't I love you better? Why is there a canyon between what I think about you, Gabriel, and how I feel when you put your arm around my waist?*

She suddenly knows the answer, and scribbles it in, even as everyone else is sending their papers up the aisles. She gives her quiz away, completed, and sighs. Gabriel now starts to raise his eyes to meet hers, and she turns away, back to the steeple, whose bronze cross at the top gleams like rock. And there, crossing the green, laughing, are Delia and Greg.

* * *

Delia and Greg realized a couple weeks ago that they have two double-free periods together, on Tuesdays and Thursdays. They usually meet in the student center, and Greg will give Delia a neck rub while they both watch CNN and argue about what's happening on the news, or Greg will scratch out English homework, while Delia wolfs an egg sandwich and distracts him with random questions and unsolicited opinions. Or, if they're beat from sports and work, they just chill, slouched on the leather couch, shins entwined.

"Shit, it's so beautiful out, though," Greg says today. "Let's take a walk, girl."

Delia looks with surprise at him—he's not really a take-a-walk guy—but then she catches a glimmer in his eye. "Take a walk where?" she says.

"Anywhere." He shrugs.

"You're feeling dirty," she says, tickling him, grinning.

"Quit it, yo," he says lazily, but acknowledging her with a wink, and then she hits his soft spot, and he squeals. For a big boy, he can be shrill like a girl. "Stop it," he says more seriously, lowering his voice, which only makes her laugh.

They walk aimlessly out the back of the school, toward the lake. They don't hold hands as they walk, already feeling conspicuous and not wanting any faculty attention. They're not doing anything wrong, technically, but they don't technically plan to do anything right either.

The grounds are manicured to the perimeter, and then velvet grass meets thigh-high golden meadow. They wade through it, pushing each other, playing. Beige crickets catapult off stems. Greg shies away: another of his girlish traits, this distaste for insects. Delia cups her hands around one and moves toward Greg.

"Dun-duh-DUN-dun," she sings.

"Get the *fuck* away, Deals, I swear to God," he says, half laughing, half dodging, quarterback-style.

Delia opens her hands, and the cricket bounces out into the blue.

They walk up a dirt path by the creek in the woods. Neither has gone far up this little road, and they're not sure what might be there. Greg puts his hand around her shoulders, her gold hair spilling over his arm.

The pines are gargantuan, blocking out sky; their branches don't begin until about twenty feet up. A green mailbox stands sentry on a drive that goes straight down, descending to the lake.

"When I was, like, ten, we were out in Utah, and my brothers went driving around these desert towns, demolishing mailboxes with a baseball bat," Delia tells him.

"C'mon, get current. Nowadays we steal Netflix."

"Oho!" she says, and doubles back as if to do that.

When Delia opens the squeaking mailbox door, the void is jammed with letters. She looks at Greg, and then she pulls out an envelope from the bottom of the stack.

"What are you doing, girl?" he asks.

"I'm looking for the postmark."

"I'm afraid to ask."

"See when they last picked up their mail. Check it out: September twentieth."

"So?"

Delia's smile grows slow and devious. "So-o-o . . . no one's here."

They hold hands and walk down the quiet, dark drive. Delia's heart is kicking. A cedar-shingled house hunches under the woods, beyond which the hill becomes vertical and they can't see anything but the glitter of water. By the door, newspapers are piled, their plastic bags damp with condensation.

She looks at Greg, his black windbreaker, his braids dark and gleaming in this forest, those baby-boy eyes. He's looking at the newspapers.

"Try it," she whispers.

He knows what she means, licks his lips, and takes two steps to the door. "This is stupid, if they leave it unlocked," he says as he squats to peer in a window. "People in my neighborhood got pit bulls guarding their homes."

Delia stands behind him, pushes him forward.

He reaches for the knob. At that moment, some bird screeches, unseen, and they both jump.

"Jesus!" Delia whispers hoarsely, a hand over her mouth to stifle laughter.

"A'ight. Here we go," Greg says. He turns the knob, the door clicks, he pushes it open.

They look at each other, radiant with bad ideas.

He takes her hand and they enter the dark foyer. She squeezes his hand hard. The house is deeply silent. The kind of quiet that only accumulates over time, like unturned pages of a calendar. Above them hangs a brass light. The home is full of dark wood furniture, shined with care, old Persian rugs that are threadbare, paintings.

They just stand in the entryway. An Asian vase on the floor is full of canes with ivory heads and umbrellas. Greg pulls her to him, and Delia presses her face against his neck, breathes in.

"We could live in a house like this," she murmurs into his skin.

He rocks her a little in response.

"I could be Mrs. Jenson, and I'd make you steak and potatoes in that kitchen, and we'd sit in front of that fire when it snowed."

They both shiver, struck by the lightning of the future. And the thrill of trespassing—in someone's home, in someone's life. Greg kisses her quickly, and he gestures to go.

"Bye, little house," Delia says as they're walking up the drive. They both know they'll come back.

* * *

Woods Crew is boring today. Nikki's supposed to be helping this senior August repair a fence, but she's not in a
teamwork frame of mind. She had a fight with Seth the
night before, because he'd been thinking about coming to
her house for Thanksgiving but his parents had convinced
him to be in La Jolla.

August keeps going on about this teacher he hates.
*Whatever, you know you'll never have the balls to say shit to his
face, so I guess you'll just waste my time with it.* Nikki holds out
tools to him like a good nurse handing over the scalpel.

In the dorm, she stops to see if Delia wants to go to dinner, because she practically never sees the girl anymore. She
opens the door, and Delia's in shorts and a windbreaker,
with muddy cleats and shin pads still on, lolling on her bed
with her phone. She holds up her finger to say she'll be off
in a second.

"Yeah, bud, it's my friend Nikki, you know, you met her
real fast. . . . Yeah, the one who was out in La Jolla visiting
Seth . . . Definitely, are you kidding, you would love her.
The question is if she would put up with you."

"Who's that?" Nikki mouths, arms crossed, smirking at
the attention.

"My bro. Mason," she answers. "What?" she now asks
into the phone. "I dunno. Dark brown hair, a hot body–"

Nikki starts laughing. "Oh my God," she says in protest.

"You should," Delia says now, and holds the phone to Nikki. "Talk to him."

Nikki makes a face of objection. "Hello," she says, shier than usual.

"Hey," a guy's voice answers, and she can tell he's smiling. "What's going on, Nikki? You taking care of my sister?"

Delia grins, knocking her cleats together.

"She doesn't really need taking care of," Nikki purrs, loving this game.

"Oh, sure she does. She's a troublemaker, how do you think she ended up a million miles from home?" He laughs.

Delia's looking closer. "What's he saying?"

"Nothing bad." Nikki laughs.

"She's the best kid," the brother is now saying, but Delia takes the phone back.

"What are you yapping about, asshole?" she says grumpily. "Yeah, whatever. Listen, bud, we got to go to dinner. I know, I know. I'm *aware*. Yeah, I'll tell her you love her," Delia says, flicking eyes in annoyance and then smiling at Nikki. "Okay, good-*bye*."

"Jesus, I'm starving," Delia says, ripping off her shirt and grabbing a towel. "Let me hit the shower real quick, then let's grab some food, okay?"

"Yeah, yeah," Nikki says, as she watches Delia walk around, barely clothed, like she owns the place.

Nikki wants to ask about the rumors; they're burning a hole in her pocket. But there's no way to bring it up.

As they cross the green, they see Somerset's tall form in the teacher's lot, talking to a redheaded woman. A lamp lights their heads and shoulders and the ground around them, but not their faces. Suddenly Somerset leans in, kisses her on the cheek. Then he points in a circle. He's either giving her directions away from school or to his house.

Delia and Nikki look at each other with surprise, then look back. The redhead gets in a car and drives away. Somerset walks in the direction of his own house. The school is a closed set, to borrow from Delia's math class, so when any unknown figure shows up on premises, there's a red alert.

The girls head inside, not speaking. They eat cheeseburgers, and halfway through, Delia says, "Let's go find out."

Nikki knows what she means. They each wrap their burgers in napkins, and eat while they walk to Somerset's.

"That bitch is trespassing," Delia says sarcastically.

"I mean, come on, right? This ain't your property, lady."

When they get near his house, the woman's car is, in fact, in the drive. The girls circle the house, at a distance, until they see them in the living room. Delia and Nikki squat under the window. Somerset is standing in front of the woman and pouring her wine.

She's pulling out the barrettes that hold her two red braids onto her head, like a German peasant. She pulls her fingers through the braids, then shakes the red hair over her shoulders. Her face is foxlike, with a pointy chin and glittering eyes—not quite pretty, but arresting. She's wearing a white knit turtleneck, and her breasts are conical, like a 1960s actress, and her beige skirt is tight around her big hips.

Somerset sits across from her at the small dining table, which is covered with stacks of papers. They're talking, he makes her laugh, and suddenly he remembers something, puts his glass down to go to the kitchen. The woman sits there, looking at her nails, and then suddenly, by some intuition—because they haven't made a noise—she looks straight at the window and into their eyes.

"Oh, shit," Nikki says, and they fall over each other, like old-fashioned comedians, as they scramble to get away from the house.

As they pant in the dorm foyer, having made it to safety, it feels like it once did, when they first started hanging out.

Delia and Greg go to the house the next week. It's a stormy day, spitting rain in the morning and staying dark through the afternoon.

They wear slickers and hold hands as they walk through the woods. Dead leaves are pasted to the ground with rainwater.

"Here's the deal. If that mail isn't there still, no way I'm going near the house," Greg says, studying the path so he doesn't trip on roots.

"Yeah, yeah," Delia says, as if acquiescing. But she won't go in either, if the mail is gone.

They see the dark shape of the house's roof just over the hill. Delia lets go of his hand to run up and pull open the mailbox. It's jammed with envelopes.

"God wants us to go into the house," she taunts him, indicating the letters with a flourish of her hand.

They shiver as they open the door, but there's that sense again, that no one has been here. Like good visitors, they take off their shoes in the foyer. Delia tiptoes around, cases the joint.

Half-charred logs in the fireplace. A basket of old newspapers. On the mantel, one picture, of a bride and groom, in black and white, from the late fifties maybe. She has false eyelashes and he's got a preppy side-part. They look scared, dizzy, young.

This is not the house Greg grew up in, and not Delia's house either.

"Check it out," Delia says, picking up recipe cards from the kitchen counter. In cursive script on a stained card is the ingredient list for raisin-walnut cookies. "I could make these for you."

"You would cook for me?"

"Yeah, if we get married."

"You think we gonna get married, Deal?"

"I'd even let you watch football all night with your boys."

"Come here, girl." Greg is sitting on a counter, and she stands between his legs and hugs him around the waist. "I would be lucky to get you for a wife. And we'll have a house eight times the size of this one. I didn't leave my whole world behind me to come to this lunatic asylum of a school for nothing. I ain't busting my ass for nothing. You watch."

She grins. Blood surges through her body. For some reason, the marriage game both quells and ignites the anxiety she feels when they're about to fool around. Or maybe it's excitement. But she loves to talk about making his bed for him and brewing his coffee and ironing his shirts.

He lowers himself down from the counter and leads her back to the living room. They sit on the couch. Interlopers. Invaders. Her takes her face in his enormous hands and kisses her, and she feels like she's wearing a wedding dress about to burst into flames.

On her way to Woods Crew, Nikki sees a couple walking far off. It looks like Greg and Delia. Her blood simmers with envy. Delia says less and less about her time with him; not only does Nikki barely see her, but she feels like she's invading when she asks about him. She feels left out when Delia *does* fill her in, and she feels left out when Delia keeps it to herself.

Nikki walks down the flagstone path. She's Jekyll and Hyde when it comes to the rumors. In a way, she wants Delia to find out that people are talking and be embarrassed. And in a way, if Delia never knows, then this belongs to Nikki—like a secret weapon. She can't admit these thoughts to herself, though.

Some dark part of her relishes the possibility that there's a video out there. The potential degradation by the community, how can that please Nikki? Does it make her feel safe that someone else will take the rap for being a girl? For being sexual? Does she want Delia to be some kind of scapegoat?

But she suddenly thinks of Delia, last afternoon. They walked to town in a fit of craving for Pop Tarts, which they could buy from the gas station store. They were on the bridge over Glendon Creek, tassels of phragmites shivering. Delia had just remembered the punch line to some dirty joke and she turned, laughing before she could even get out the funny part, and squeezed Nikki's arm with her big hand. Nikki had looked at her almost German features—big and warm and open. Who could ever hurt this girl? Who could stand for it?

Nikki's almost to the Woods Crew Suburban that takes

them out to the site. Kids are grouped around it in Shetland sweaters and gloves and fleeces. Is she honestly jealous? It's funny, she never even considered Greg, *that way*, until Delia did. His china-white eyes, with the ebony pupils and girlish lashes. When Delia started liking him, shit, she doesn't know—it's like he started then to exist as a sexual being.

When Delia does her replay of one of their hook-ups, Nikki's forced to imagine things. She doesn't want to know any of it, and yet she wants to know all of it, and she can't meet Delia's eyes when they talk about it.

"What's up, mama?" Parker says now, flinging pine needles at Nikki, who's reached the group.

"Hola," Nikki answers, so guilty and shamefaced—without even knowing what she's been thinking about really—that she blushes.

11

Nikki and Parker are unzipping their coats as they enter their room, laughing about how Grant had done a jig on a bet today. The phone in the room is ringing. It's Seth.

"Whoa," Nikki says, not having expected him. They usually only talk about once a week, and they talked a couple nights ago. "What's up, baby?"

"Nothing," he says, in this slow, testy way that means something's up. "How *you* doing?"

"All's good, I guess. Just got back from Woods Crew, had a funny day out there. I swear to God that—"

"Listen. I just want to bring something out in the open, you know? I heard some shit, and that's all. Just want to bring it up."

Nikki says "okay" in a dull voice, looks at Parker, who

heads to the common room.

"So, are you sort of hanging around that Colombian dude?"

"Gabriel?"

"I guess."

"We're friends," Nikki says. "But I haven't, I mean, I'm not going to. You know."

He clears his throat. "I mean, I hope not." He laughs bitterly. "I'm not trying to, like, police you, but someone told me you guys were hanging out."

"Not like that," she says, hoping by all her vagueness to escape feeling like she lied.

"Oh, for Christ's sake." He sighs, his voice distant.

"What?" she says, her mouth dry.

He changes his tone. "Nothing, Nik. If that's what you say, that's what I have to believe."

"Okay-y-y," Nikki says, faltering.

"So I'll talk to you later."

"Okay! Catch you later!" she says.

Then she lies back on the bed. *"Catch you later"? What am I, on a bad high-school sitcom? Who says that? Fucking nobody says that.*

It's Thursday. Greg and Delia missed the last double-free they had together because Greg had to meet with Mr. Terrazi to talk about a paper. It's a shiny day, the sky squeaky blue. Delia goes running ahead of him, her pants catching on brambles. She's euphoric and terrified. They've almost had sex a few times, but didn't quite get there. Today they're going to go through with it, and in a bed, in a house. The way it should be. Care of the bride and groom on the mantel, their innkeepers.

"Yo, Deals, you gotta slow down. My hamstring is all tore up," Greg says, ambling through the weeds.

Delia looks at him, his broad shoulders, his big hand catching at the chaff of the tall grasses. Sun gleaming off his obsidian cheekbones. Denim thighs whispering as his legs brush against each other. Sometimes she has to look away from him because he's too much.

When he catches up to her at the mailbox, she bows her head, suddenly shy, her hands clasped in front of her. He smooths her hair down and pulls her to him. They're both nervous.

"Do I get the honor?" he asks, gesturing at the mailbox. She nods.

He opens it. It's packed.

Inside, they proceed to the bedroom in silence. Take off their shoes, looking at each other. The light that makes it through the pines is green, and it filters through the bedroom drapes to pattern the ivory duvet. Greg takes his shirt off, and she looks at the trail of black hair that starts in the center of his chest and thins to nothing on his hard stomach, starts again above his waistband.

"What do you think," he whispers. "Under the covers?"

"Hell, yes," she whispers back. "I want it to be real."

He pulls back the duvet. "Not sure what that has to do with the covers, Deal, but I'm gonna go with it."

They laugh and this breaks the brittle ice. They've taken off everything but underwear, and they slide into the bed clumsily, awkwardly. But when her bare stomach meets his, the warmth melts her fears, and suddenly she can't get as close to him as she wants. She's holding him hard and still wants to be closer.

Eventually he hangs an arm over the side of the bed, fumbles in his pants' pockets until he finds it. Tears the package with his teeth while she lies back, heart double-pounding. Toward the end, she starts to feel the rustle, then the chaos she's felt before at this moment. It's love, and pleasure, and the terror that it will be taken away one day. She cries, like a kitten—whimpering, desperate—as Greg says her name and shudders.

He kisses her neck after, wipes a tear moving down her cheek in slow motion. "Did I hurt you?" he asks.

She shakes her head on the pillow. But he did. He didn't mean to. And he didn't hurt her physically. *Christ, what is it? What do I feel right now?* He opened up a space in her and it will be empty unless he stays with her.

They get up, abruptly mortal, aware of their bodies, the

bodies they lost in the last half hour. Delia jokes about not being able to find her underwear and they laugh. When they're dressed, Greg helps Delia make the bed, but he's not natural at it, and she tells him he's a bad homemaker and he should go put on his shoes. He leaves her in the bedroom, and she pulls the sheets tight first, then arranges the duvet.

She's plumping the pillows when he tears back in and grabs her hand. He has her shoes. Hoarsely, viciously: "They're *out* there."

Delia doesn't have time to ask anything because he pulls her into the kitchen. They get to the kitchen where there's a back door, and he fumbles with the lock. Delia hears a pair of voices. *Oh my God. Oh my holy God.* Greg opens the kitchen door, and they proceed delicately so they won't be heard on the other side. As they step out and close the door, the voices stop. The man asks something, and the woman answers, but Delia can't hear what they're saying.

"C'mere," Greg says, pulling her down an embankment, thick with young pines, and she almost laughs as they skid down one decline after another. They make it to the lakeshore, which is tricky with smooth stones. They hop over them, twisting their ankles, and Delia wishes they could slow down, but Greg is still running like a maniac.

"Can we slow down?" she whispers loudly.

He doesn't answer, just picks up the pace.

Finally, after twenty minutes, her breath ragged and her ankles cut, she forces Greg to stop. *"Please,"* she says again.

He looks back where the house would be but it's too far to see anything, and after a minute of hyperventilating, his shoulders drop. She bends, hands on her knees, and laughs. He doesn't join in, but when she stands and puts her arms around him, he holds her.

It's only later, when she tells Nikki about it, laughing and glowing with the near miss, that she understands.

Nikki reminds her of the basic facts. "*You* would have been in some trouble, but do you know what it would mean for Greg? Black kid caught in a white house in Connecticut? It's not the same, Deal. It's a good thing you got out of there."

"I never thought of that," she says. And she loves Greg more now, for being brave enough to deal with this dimension of the issue by himself. She gets that pang: of love, and fear of love. It's the same feeling.

Nikki feels like a suspect, ducking through the crowds of students, in their tweed and wool and fleece, who are walking on paths from one academic building to the other. She glances fearfully at the sky, as though Seth's head, like some sun god, might be glaring down on her unfaithful ass. *But I haven't done anything,* she whines in her own head. *What does he expect from me?* This is her favorite: *I've been better than*

136

some girls would be. He should be grateful. When she uses up those well-worn justifications, she performs a magnificent feat of irrationality, and swings the whole situation around so that Gabriel is to blame for everything.

Somerset sees Delia and Nikki sitting in the sun after chapel one day. It's in the fifties, not warm, but warm enough to soak up something. They're kicking their heels against the brick wall.

"Well, it's the CIA," he says.

They both look at him.

"My spies," he continues, and he sounds angry. "Well, not quite mine. You're spying *on* me, not for me."

Delia and Nikki look at each other, stricken. So the redhead tattled.

"Um, we can explain that," Nikki says.

He crosses his arms. "Oh, you can?"

"Delia can," Nikki says, nudging her friend.

Delia opens her mouth in alarm at Nikki, and Nikki suddenly starts laughing, and then Delia does, and Somerset—as bad and tough as he wants to look—can't hold it in either.

"Who is she anyway, Somer?" Delia asks, her confidence back and even sharpened now.

"Never would have put you with a redhead," Nikki adds, thrilled, as she knows that she and Delia are once again pushing the envelope.

"Didn't know you were placing bets. She's an old friend."

"Oh, really? An 'old friend'? We know what that means, we're not kids," Delia scoffs. "What's your friend's name?"

"Not that it's your business, but her name is Hannah."

"Well," says Delia conspiratorially. "You can do better than Hannah."

"Gee, thanks," Somerset says. "But you don't know her. Hannah apparently can do better than me."

"What do you mean, she dumped you?" Nikki says, aware that she's crossing a line.

Somerset looks away.

Delia nudges Nikki. "Dude, I'm sorry," she blurts out.

"Yeah, I'm sorry," Delia says with a straight face too.

Somerset is moving away from them with an air of regret. "Whatever," he says, waving them away.

When he's gone, the girls clutch each other's arms. They're four-fifths sincerity, one-fifth melodrama. *Their poor little Somerset! Hannah doesn't want him!* Delia puts her hands over her mouth and shakes her head in exaggerated pity.

"Can you *believe* it?" Nikki says.

Somehow being able to feel sorry for him this way charges both girls with a feeling of power, of dominance. They sit on the wall, kicking it with their heels, slouched but with faces turned up to the sky in lazy and confident defiance.

12

Saturday morning is gray, lacking any sense of promise—
even though it is, in fact, chock-full of promise. No one
wakes up excited. The fact that Saturday classes exist saps
hope for ever *feeling* a real weekend. They move from classroom to classroom, taking notes on lunar gas or
Dostoyevsky or rape as a weapon of war in Africa. They
watch the minute hand on the clock dragging across the
face of the morning like a rusty razor.

It's only when they walk out of their last class of the
morning, hurrying to their dorms to pack, that Nikki,
Parker, Delia, and Gabriel realize, separately, they're getting
off campus. They're going to Head of the Charles, the
regatta on the Boston river that magnetically attracts the
preppy universe to its banks.

Delia's the last to arrive at the bus that's taking about thirty Wellington students there. She's dragging her duffel on the grass, a Twizzler hanging out of her mouth like a cigarette, her coat off one shoulder like she's in the middle of a striptease. That's Delia, always discombobulated in a glamorous tomboy way.

"Yee-ha!" she says, high-fiving down the aisle like a rock star.

She sits next to Parker, throws her bag under the seat. She's beaming. "Where's Greg?"

Parker peers at her own hair, which she's braiding. "I heard his game is running way late, he sent a message with Gabe," she says, then looks up apologetically.

Gabriel and Nikki share the seat across. Nikki leans over Gabriel's lap, her breasts hanging out of her Juicy Couture shirt. "Did Parker just tell you that Greg can't make it?"

"What?" Delia spits out in an ugly way.

"I'm sorry, Deals," Nikki says.

"I can't believe this," she says. She'd been looking forward to this weekend to the exclusion of being able to think about anything else. Delia's eyes brim; she feels that ferocious anger when you're little and drop your just-bought ice-cream cone on the sand. She's embarrassed, and looks past Parker out the window. "I don't even want to go now."

"You've got *us*," Nikki says, still leaning toward Delia.

And Delia has to restrain from snarling at her. She feels

like Nikki's taunting her, and stays turned to the window.

Over the hours, she watches cattle farms roll by, the black Angus regal and motionless in wide fields. A mahogany horse nuzzling a white horse. Strings of houses, small and mediocre, that refuse to give any clue as to what goes on inside: happiness, abuse, devotion. They're in the slow lane of the thruway, passed by cars and trucks, most now with Massachusetts plates. Green signs announce towns they're passing, places Delia will never know.

She's watching it all and seeing none of it. All she can see is Greg slouching at the snack bar, against the soda machine, chewing on a straw. Jackie Hargrove is praising his touchdown today, and now she's asking where in Brooklyn he grew up, because she grew up in New York City, and now they're laughing and she's way too close.

Or it's Madeline Dux, her black bangs hiding her eyes— sitting with Greg at a dining hall table where they somehow ended up alone. Or Keisha Sanson-Briggs, offering a bite of her grilled cheese in her aggressive way, but this time he sees something new in Keisha that he never saw with Delia around.

The sun breaks through the gray sky in Boston. They're wandering the city, having met Delia's aunt Molly and dropping their bags at the house, broken off from the Wellington crew. The cobblestones are rosy with sunset.

"Check it out," Nikki says, licking oil off her finger from a bag of hot peanuts and pointing. "You know that guy, Park. He was chatting you up at the Gold and Silver, remember?"

Parker adjusts her glasses, long hair swirling behind her like a cape. "Oh yeah. That dude from Holderness."

The bearded guy wears a lumberjack shirt and a cap. He's one of many, as the streets are thronged today with prep-schoolers and former boarding-school kids now at colleges. Everyone looks familiar; they're archetypal silhouettes.

Delia reaches into Nikki's vellum bag of hot peanuts, throws a few back. "Everyone here knows everyone else." She's pulled it together a bit and is trying to have fun, as if her thoughts aren't laser-focused on what Greg is doing. She feels the familiar urge to check text messages. She's already beaten herself up for forgetting her phone.

It's true, no one gets far, as crowds surge, without clapping someone on the back, introducing friends. They smile and laugh as they trade the latest, worst, best stories of their lives tucked away in these tiny worlds.

The crew stand on the stone bridge and look down as the sculls roll by, burning up the water, the rowers' bodies timed like an orchestra. The city is classical, Delia thinks. Not like California, where everyone is young and free, even when they're old. This is a place of books and universities and rules and maps and ports. She can see ghosts of tea party ships sinking in the harbor.

And here she is, standing at its historical center. Watching a race. The sun making the cobblestones gleam like black teeth. She's embedded in a preppy mafia.

She looks at Parker, who's leaning over the side of the bridge, enchanted. Her profile, her hair knotted at the back of her head, her black military coat hanging in tatters to the tops of her violet boots. *I would never know her if everything hadn't happened in my life the way it did. I would not have Parker as a friend.* She measures this in her head against having left home, having left home the way she did, all of it. She puts both lumps in scales in her mind, and they equal each other's weight.

"Look," Parker says, beckoning Delia closer.

"What is it?" Delia asks.

It's a scattering of roses in the water, white flowers that shine like fish. "Those girls just threw them over," Parker says, happy at this small incident.

The scales tip.

There's no way to avoid the exhilaration. As twilight claims the city's riverbanks and its alleys, the excitement of the racers gets transferred to the spectators. Mobs swarm the brownstone-lined streets, where boutique windows are still lit up, and restaurants and bars are deepening and getting louder.

"What should we do?" Delia asks, walking backward so she can talk to her group.

"Does *anyone* have a fake ID?" Nikki asks.

They all shake their heads. Eventually, they court Hamilton College guys outside a package store to buy pints of Jack Daniel's and Captain Morgans. They transfer these into emptied Coke bottles, storing one in Parker's handbag and one in Nikki's. Earlier that day, a group from Exeter said to go to Mulligan's Pub on Bay Street, which is a restaurant as well as a bar, so they can actually get in. Boston is hard on under-agers.

"We have to be home by ten-thirty," Delia confesses, as they eat cheeseburgers at the pub tables. "My aunt is kind of strict, and there's just no way I can get in trouble with her. We negotiated a little, and that's all I can do."

Parker smiles at Delia, who's been dreading telling them this. "No worries, seriously. We're here, we're off campus, it's all good."

Nikki nods and smiles, but her mood is uneven. There's guys everywhere and she's burdened with Gabriel. He keeps looking at her in that way, like he's not supposed to look at her and is embarrassed by his own face. There's a posse at the next table, the guys with arms around blond girls, in Barbour coats, patched jeans, with Ray-Bans dangling off Croakies, hair messy after a day of running and celebrating and drinking, wild eyes. *I want to be at that table.*

Nikki decides to get tipsy, to take the edge off. She winks at Parker, and they go to the bathroom to nip from their contraband bottles. The minute the girls leave, Delia asks for Gabriel's phone again. She mouths "sorry" to him, takes the phone outside.

The street is colder now, and she hunches her shoulders as the phone rings and rings. She hangs up and dials again. A woman walks a Dalmatian, and two guys, standing outside Mulligan's to smoke, bend to pet the dog. Suddenly a very sleepy Noah answers the phone.

"What?" he croaks.

"Noah, where's Greg, it's Deals."

There's sniffling, a rustling of sheets. "Dude, I was sleeping, why do you have to keep calling like that?"

"Where is he?"

"Where do you think, Deals? I don't know, eating or playing Ping-Pong. Shit, I don't even know what time it is."

Delia tries her sweet voice. "Hey, babe, would you just do me a favor? Can you just check really quickly if he's out in the hall, or in the bathroom?"

Noah groans, doesn't answer.

"Please, babe. I know I can count on you."

"Oh, Christ," he says, and she hears noises that indicate he's going to look. Her mind whirs. She needs to talk to him; it's an animal necessity.

"Deals," Noah says, exasperated. "I checked the floor,

the john, I even knocked on Simms's door. Nada. He's just at the snack bar or something. He's fucking starved. He played a game in the rain."

"Did they win?"

"Yeah."

"Tell him to call me at this number, it's Gabe's phone. Are you going to see him?"

"Delia, I don't *know*."

She's passed a line and scrambles to make it up. "Okay, kid. Sorry to bother you, I just miss you guys!"

"Well, have fun, Deals. Say hi to everyone," Noah says, conciliatory too.

Delia, fiery-eyed, asks one of the guys for a smoke. He bumps a Camel Light from the pack and she pulls it out. She's no quitter. His buddy lights it for her with a match.

"Hey, I'm Delia."

Aaron and Jeremiah shake her hand in turn. They're at Babson, they're sophomores. When she tells them she's at Wellington, Aaron asks if she knows Caroline Camper. Jeremiah went to Salisbury and asks if she knows people who graduated Wellington a couple years ago.

"No, I just got there. Just this year."

"Where you from?" Aaron asks.

"La Jolla."

"You're a long way from home, Delia," Jeremiah says, exhaling smoke from his nose. "Can't imagine leaving the beach for these crappy winters. You must be a glutton for pain."

"Yeah, what brought you east?" Aaron asks.

Delia gives them a dazzling smile and takes a drag. "God, I don't know. Just plain old wanderlust, I guess," she lies.

When she brings her new friends inside, she has the air of a cat who caught two mice. She gives Gabriel his phone. Her new friends drag her to the bar, and she drinks a Diet Coke while they order beers. Part of her listens to them, and the rest of her waits for Greg to call. Aaron orders a Patrón shot, and she does it out of the bartender's sight. Her mouth is on fire. She licks the flames off her lips and smiles at the boys.

13

The night is fun. Nikki gets rum in her and loosens up. Groups meld, merge, separate, dissolve. The wiseguys and show-offs jump like monkeys, slamming shots, knocking into one another. Parker talks near the jukebox with a kid in overalls, and Delia's the centerpiece of a group of guys. Jeremiah has her ear, though, telling her some story. Nikki looks over at her; Delia's got her hand on the small of his back.

"Are you having a good time?" Gabriel asks Nikki.

"Don't I look like I'm having a good time?"

"Well, excuse me for asking."

"For the record, it's better to have a good time and not talk about it. You know what I mean?" As usual, Nikki's being rude and he doesn't deserve it. She wants to be here with Delia, alone, so they can make trouble. There's *so* many guys here, and she's saddled with the nice one.

He shrugs, sips his doctored ginger ale, adjusts his face so that everything is okay. Nikki feels bad. She pulls at his arm affectionately, suggests they go out so he can smoke.

"Cool," he says. "Lead the way."

They find the alley behind Mulligan's. The ground glitters, mica in the asphalt.

Gabriel lights a Red, and Nikki has a drag even though she quit. The smokers are boisterous, charismatic. A hippie kid is dancing and cracking everyone up. His hair is long, frizzy, the cuffs of his jeans long and ragged. He's got on an L.L.Bean sweater and gloves, no jacket.

"Hey, you lovebirds got a light?" the hippie kid asks, dancing near them.

"Sure," Gabriel says while Nikki looks away.

A friend of theirs stumbles out of the bar, with a tumbler of whiskey. "Fuck, dude, I'm kicked. Someone take this."

"We're going to jet, Mackenzie, let's go. Put it down."

The new guy looks with bleary red eyes at Nikki and Gabriel, and Nikki smiles, grabs the drink from him. "I'll take it."

"That's my girl," the guy slurs, like a drunken father.

The group leaves, trailing marijuana smoke. Nikki takes a searing sip.

"Cheers!" Nikki says, taking a bigger sip, then screwing up her face. "Whoa."

She gives Gabriel a sip, holding the glass for him. Gabriel puts an arm around her as he shakes his head from the liquor. *"Damn."*

And suddenly two cops are standing in front of them. Gabriel grabs the drink from Nikki and puts it on a stone ledge. Nikki almost throws up from fear. The cops are prototypes of Boston police, one with a red mustache, the other with sad, careless blue eyes.

Red Mustache shakes his head. "You kids have a good time at the old Head of the Charles today?"

Nikki and Gabriel look at each other. Gabriel answers yes.

Blue Eyes smiles. "Yeah, it's a good time, a good old time. You're not from here, are you?"

Red Mustache nods at the whiskey on the ledge. "Bad idea, son. Real bad idea."

"I'm sorry, officer. Someone came out of the bar and handed it to us, and we put it there on the ledge. That's all that happened."

Blue Eyes: "Actually, I think I saw your girlfriend drink from it."

"She didn't, sir."

"I imagine you kids are far from twenty-one," Mustache says.

Nikki's head reels. They'll have to get Delia's aunt to handle this, and then Wellington might find out, and all their parents will go crazy. Her father will not understand.

"Neither of us is twenty-one, sir." Gabriel answers. Suddenly the alley seems tiny, glittering with menace.

Blue Eyes mimes pity. "Hate to do this, but you kids are going to have to come with me."

Gabriel takes out his wallet. "Sir, can I ask you to look at this?"

Both cops look at the card Gabriel unfolds. Nikki has no idea what it is. The cops look at each other. Blue Eyes' face is turning mottled red around the jowls, like marbled steak.

Mustache hands it back with a soldier's crispness. "I'm not going to say anything further." The way he says it says everything. And Gabriel takes it without blinking.

Gabriel puts his arm around Nikki's quaking shoulders and escorts her to the ladies' room, where she stands inside a stall and tries to breathe.

When she returns to their table, Gabriel is signing the bill. She looks at him like a kid looks at a stranger who pulls her out of a fire.

"What the hell was that?" she asks.

"My diplomatic immunity card."

"Your diplo-what?"

"My get-out-of-jail-free card."

Suddenly Parker swoops down on them. "God, where were you guys?"

"Just outside, having a smoke," Gabriel says.

"And almost getting arrested," Nikki says, but Parker isn't paying attention. "Although Gabriel flashed his international superstar badge and got us out of it."

"Whoa. I suddenly realized I was alone here and got really freaked out, I don't even know what neighborhood we're staying in."

"Well, Delia's still in here," Nikki says.

"No, she's not. I've looked everywhere. I didn't think about it until I realized you guys were missing too. I thought you were all together."

Nikki and Gabriel look at each other.

"Um, no," Nikki says. "I haven't seen her."

"Do you think she left with those guys?" Parker says in a voice that manages to withhold judgment.

Nikki shrugs, but a cascade of bad images clicks through her head: Delia in a hotel room, Delia in a car, a guy holding back her hair, a guy telling her what to do, a guy whose name she can't remember, a guy who isn't Greg.

"Let's walk to her aunt's," Nikki says, her stomach sinking. "We'll leave a note with the bartender that we checked out. Let's get back."

Gabriel thinks he knows where it is and they start walking. Each corner they turn looks like the last: brick, unknowable, lamplit. All the celebration they'd enjoyed is now erratic, the groups they pass in the dark are aggro, and they notice puke in the gutter more than once.

"This is it," Gabriel says, as they come upon the town house.

Nikki would have walked right by it. The three of them look at one another. Gabriel has the house phone number, but they're worried they'll wake up the Brownes.

Suddenly a curtain is moved aside, then let drop. Delia throws open the front door.

"Holy shit," she whispers loudly. "Where have you guys *been*? Jesus, I thought I lost you."

Nikki stares at Delia, trying to see through her, or into her. "What do you mean? *You* lost *us*, you left us at Mulligan's."

"What are you *talking* about? I looked around and no one was there. I was the only one of us still there."

"When did you leave?" Nikki asks.

Delia doesn't like the flavor of this. She stands on the stoop, flanked by black iron railings. Her pajama pants shiver and her feet are bare. She's on trial. "I don't know the exact *time* when I left, but I've been home for more than forty-five minutes. Do you have any other questions? Because I've been waiting up for you guys, and I'm ready to go to bed."

Her last words are icy. She turns, walks inside, hurt and stoic.

Delia's taken a tiny third-story room that was once a servant's quarters. Her lights are out, and her eyes have adjusted to make out the bones of the room. The molding. The legs of the bedside table. The lamp. Her luggage is lumped on the floor, clothes strewn from it like garbage a raccoon takes from a pail.

She wonders what life was like for the maid who once lived here. Who woke up and went to sleep alone in this chamber. Who lived with the family but did not belong to them.

Shit, where on earth am I? Delia loved her Peter Pan book when she was a kid, and she thinks now of when the kids floated out of their beds into the night. If she could do that now, she'd coast out in some mystical nightgown into the Boston sky, and take off to California. Grab some enchiladas and Tecate, find a drum circle in some backyard where boys throw sticks for big dogs in the dark, and beautiful girls make out with each other. She would skinny-dip in someone else's pool. Smoke some San Diego weed. Fall asleep eating Ben & Jerry's Cherry Garcia on a regular couch in a regular den in a regular house.

Nikki and Delia don't talk about Boston until the next Sunday. They talk around it, and when people ask about the weekend, they each give a tourist's account of a sunny day by the river, and a night drinking on the town.

Delia now knows that rumors are spreading. The way Gabriel, Parker, and Nikki looked up the stone steps at her that night. She thinks she's being paranoid, and at the same time she knows she's right. From room to room, a Morse code of gossip is being tapped on the walls: *Delia is a bad girl, Delia is a bad girl.* She overdresses, as if wearing more clothes could protect her. One evening, in a baseball cap, hood pulled over it, oversized jeans, and basketball sneakers, she crosses the green to the library like a blond gangster. In algebra, she has to be asked to take off her coat midway through class.

Maybe she should send out a newsletter, set the record straight. Like Mark Twain: "The news of my death has been greatly exaggerated." But here we come to the question, which was number four on Mr. Ryan's English quiz yesterday, of whether or not these reports are exaggerated. Did she die a little bit? Should she put some element of herself in a coffin, lay white lilies on the gleaming wooden box, and lower it into the ground? If she died a little, could she get reborn a little more?

Talk. Talk talk. She hears it now. As she spoons Jell-O from the salad bar basin into a bowl, or changes into her soccer shorts in the locker room. Talk. Like little birds who see the sun rising—every single day the same sun—and are still compelled to chatter about it.

But it's Nikki, of course, who upsets Delia the most.

"If I hunted down mountain bikes, would you take a ride with me later?" Delia asks now, a week after their return. She's poked her head into Nikki's room, woken her up. It's noon.

Nikki rubs her eyes. "Sure."

They borrow bikes from Dr. Thielssen. The girls stand and pedal up the inclines, and then coast down curves through the dark, cold woods. The air going into their lungs is minty, even silver. Nikki has a hard time keeping up, but when they finally stop to get their breath, the endorphins catch up.

They rub their hands to get blood moving, and stare at the lake. It looks almost black in this weather.

"Can I, like . . . Do you mind if I ask you something?" Delia says.

Nikki shrugs, knowing what they're about to discuss.

"What did you think I did the other night, in Boston?" Delia looks at her friend aggressively. "Did you think I would ever, like, not come straight home?"

"I don't know. You were hanging out with that guy Jeremiah."

"Yeah, I was, but in case you didn't notice, I've been going out with Greg."

Nikki breaks a twig from the bush. She continues to break it into sections.

"I'm a loyal person," Delia says, and her voice cracks.

Nikki's shocked to see the shimmer of tears. She decides to ask. "Did you have to leave La Jolla?"

Delia stares at Nikki. "What did you hear? You obviously heard something."

"That you got together, with . . . that you and some guys from the football team . . ."

Delia laughs sharply. "Lie."

"That you and your best friend and her boyfriend, on the beach . . ."

"Lie. These are rumors, Nik."

Nikki now looks at Delia, whose face is desperate and earnest. "Oh my God, Delia." She moves to hug her friend, and smells the shampoo of her hair, patchouli on her hot neck, sweat. "I'm sorry."

"You are my one real friend here, Nik. *Please* stop second-guessing me. I won't ever do that to you."

"I'm sorry I was an asshole."

"No, it's okay, just please . . ."

"I know."

Delia looks over Nikki's shoulder as she waits for the crying urge to subside. Across the lake is the house that she and Greg sneaked into. She has never seen it from this perspective, and it looks so beautiful and natural, as if it grew there, like a toadstool. She sniffles, and then sighs. The windows are dark, but she knows what's inside.

14

Winter is creeping like ice crystals over the school. Work is intensifying. Rooms get stale, with no windows open. Everyone turns to macaroni and cheese, or chocolate, or the bland apple pie they serve in the dining hall, looking for comfort and warmth.

Nikki and Delia hang out in the Penthouse Suite. They look out the window at this place called *Elsewhere*, or *Outside*, or *The Free World*. One day they watch a Coca-Cola truck drive in all its red-and-white glory to the depot of the cafeteria.

"Shit, forget the whole weekend sign-out parental-permission thing. We could be stowaways in there," Delia says, painting her toenails fuchsia instead of finishing her math work sheet.

This becomes one of their regular jokes, this old-fashioned idea of breaking out. Throwing a line of knotted sheets out the window. Burying themselves in laundry. Whittling a spoon into a shank. Raiding the vending machine for Butterfingers and Mountain Dew, stowing them in a hobo's bandanna pouch on a stick, and striking out for adventure.

"Yeah, dude, but where would we go?" Nikki laughs. "Glendon has, like, three places open. We could go get chop suey, buy some scratch-offs at the gas station, and check out a book from the public library. Yee-ha."

"Connecticut. It's a wasteland," Delia says wistfully. "Pure desert."

After Nikki leaves, Delia tries to do math but she pictures Greg at practice instead, his face burning inside his white cage of a helmet. Geese crossing the aquamarine sky above him. He squirts water toward his mouth, and it wets his shirt around the neck. His boys clap him on the back.

That's the Greg she worships. The other half of him is still a kid. He walks around the buildings with one shoe untied, laces dragging, until a teacher nags him. Pages flutter down from the messy stack of notebooks and textbooks under his arm. He clings to her when he's procrastinating, playing with her fingers at the snack bar. Singing hip-hop songs in a falsetto, saying her name over and over, anything to avoid dealing with his workload. He asks if he can have the other half of her sandwich. He slurps the end of his orange soda.

It's the childish yin to the yang of his heroic self. The Greg who's got black wings sprouting from his number 8 jersey, and golden feet. The noble Greg. Whose soul is so all-encompassing, especially when they fool around—hot bodies on a cold marble floor—that she can't see her way out of him. She has to be nice to the juvenile Greg in order to stay tight with the magnificent Greg.

The sun shines that Sunday. Nikki wonders what Delia has up her sleeve. *Is this another one of her surprises, like apple picking and birthday parties?* Earlier that morning, after Parker left for the studio, Delia burst into her room and insisted she and Gabriel join her and Greg on a "religious session" in the woods.

"Listen, since none of us go to church, I figure we need some spirituality on a Sunday."

"Delia, Gabriel is a practicing Catholic," Nikki responded. "He's probably in confession right now."

"Whatever. He's coming anyway."

Nikki prefers the woods thick; in crisp, late November, the naked trees make her feel exposed. Delia won't tell where they're headed, but finally they reach Amsterdam cabin. Nikki knows this place well, having reshingled its roof during Woods Crew last year. Two old couches, one covered in skanky cream tweed and the other in threadbare blue velvet. Black smudges mar the pale stone fireplace. A mildewed Trivial Pursuit box is in the corner.

Inside, Greg, Delia, and Nikki lounge while Gabriel throws wood into the fireplace and tries, unsuccessfully, to get a fire going.

"Hey, Eagle Scout, you ever light a fire in Colombia?" Delia heckles from the couch. "Step aside, Nature Boy." Delia hip-bumps Gabriel, leans down, and makes a tepee with kindling. She lights newspaper underneath and blows until twigs crackle.

"Check you out," Greg says.

"Troop 149, La Jolla. I also sold more cookies than my entire troop, thank you very much."

"I smell bullshit." Nikki smiles. "How many did your dad buy?"

"Put it this way. We weren't going to starve because of a lack of Thin Mints."

Delia brushes her hands on her thighs. She reaches into her corduroy jacket pocket, tosses a Ziploc baggie on the table.

"What's that?" Nikki asks.

"A Tijuana care package from my brother. I told you we were going on a spiritual trip today. You guys hungry?"

Nikki and Gabriel look at each other with big eyes. "Oh my God!" Nikki says, hand over her mouth, grinning with temptation. Nikki immediately decides she's in, although she's only eaten crumbs from someone else's trip once before.

"I've never done shrooms." Gabriel inspects the bag, his face betraying curiosity as much as anxiety.

"G, it's cool. Just pop a cap and a stem. It won't wig you out. I've done it a couple times," Greg says.

"Pop a cap? Am I supposed to shoot someone?" Gabriel says wryly.

"Just don't eat a lot, fatso." Delia grins. "Plus, Nikki's here to take care of you in case you freak out." Delia opens the bag and divides the shriveled, ridged shrooms into four piles. "All right, guys, dig in."

"No peanut butter?" Nikki looks at Delia.

"Come on, Nik. Be a big girl."

"But isn't it like grown under cow shit?" Nikki tosses a cap in her mouth, shudders. "This tastes like cardboard," she says, chewing slowly.

"Yeah, very dirty cardboard." Gabriel is digging a piece of stem from his molar.

Greg and Delia take their time eating through the piles. They tap two stems together like champagne glasses and toast, "To no regrets."

Once the shrooms are gone, everyone settles into the couches. The fire and the anticipation heat the room quickly. They start yawning, and Nikki says her teeth feel weird.

"It's coming on," Delia says with a wicked grin.

The first rush sloshes through the room. Time swells

and contracts. Yesterday and tomorrow evaporate. They're dazed and confused.

Ideas are strung like Christmas lights in Nikki's head. One by one they blink, then pop, leaving smoke. She sees a frog, but it's a rock, and she laughs, delighted by this trick. She looks around, sure that everyone saw the stone frog, or maybe she already announced it. She's not sure what she's thinking or what she's saying. They all spend a while in this stone-frog zone, looking at the world as if all its objects just crystallized out of fog: the leaves decomposing on the sill of the window, the potato bug like a prehistoric insect traveling a seam on the floor, the lake glittering like fire beyond the door.

When the first wave breaks, Delia hops up, announces they're going to explore.

The midday sun startles the group and their pupils dilate. Delia picks up a yellow leaf. "Check out this leaf. I hope I'm this beautiful when I die." Delia grabs dirt and smears it onto her arm.

"That's like *Apocalypto*," Gabriel announces randomly.

Nikki laughs but Gabriel thinks he's onto something.

"The Mayan civilization was on some serious junk, you know?"

Delia picks up leaves and throws them.

Nikki picks up her own pile and stuffs it down Delia's jacket. They make a leaf pile, and jump into it like they're ten, not aware of bruising and cutting themselves. They laugh so hard it hurts.

"Come on, let's go extreme walking." Delia pulls Greg's arm and they all head down one of the trails.

Everything is complex, the oak tree's roots breaking from the dirt like a hand. Or it's luscious, like moss on a sapling. To Nikki, these woods radiate power, and she's careful what she touches, as if she could be electrocuted.

Greg discovers a stream, glutted with leaves but moving. "You know, sometimes the hardest thing in life is to swim against the current."

Delia thinks he's kidding, but his wide glassy eyes are earnest.

Nikki uncharacteristically puts her arm around Gabriel's waist and snuggles into his chest. When she looks up, she notices his eyes. She can see every sliver of brown and gold.

"You have beautiful eyes. You know that?"

"Thanks, Nik." Gabriel kisses Nikki on the forehead.

Suddenly she's terrified of his affection, and tears away, acting playful. He runs after her. Delia and Greg chase too, as if this is a game, but Nikki feels hunted down. They're running, dodging branches and squealing, until Nikki whirls around and yells for them to stop. She's panting in the new silence.

Delia and Greg look at each other, and then at Gabriel.

"You okay, Nik?" Delia asks.

Nikki heaves, her palm still up to halt them all from getting closer.

"I want to make an announcement," Gabriel says.

Delia claps. "Yay!"

Gabriel points at Nikki. "I love this girl."

Nikki recoils. Delia registers her fear and pulls Gabriel and Nikki near her, an arm over each one's shoulder. "Gabe, you are the sweetest. Nikki, isn't he?"

Nikki stares. She can't handle this.

Delia holds her tighter. "Now, we are all tripping our *faces* off, and that is lovely and wonderful. We *all* love each other so much. Right, Greg?" She makes a meaningful face at Greg to come join them. They all hug.

Gabriel is sweating now. "Did I say something wrong?"

"Naw, man," Greg says. "You said everything right. Didn't he, Nikki? We all love each other, don't we, Nikki? We're all best friends."

Nikki looks to Greg for reassurance and then to Delia again. Finally she looks at Gabe, whose face is afraid. "I love all you guys," Nikki says in a hushed whisper.

"Yay!" Delia says again, and breaks free to dance in the leaves, the crisis passed.

They follow the stream farther, and it splits a few times and they finally decide to turn back before they get too lost. The energy is starting to sparkle out. On their way back to the cabin, Gabriel sees something dart through the woods.

"Guys, I just saw a mountain lion."

Greg is explaining to Gabriel how there are no mountain lions, when he sees it too. "Holy shit, man. What the hell is that?"

"That's not a mountain lion, fellas. It's a Golden Retriever." Nikki points at the dog, visible through bare trees. All of a sudden, it hits them. *Dogs mean faculty*.

Delia suggests splitting up. "It'll be less suspicious."

Gabriel and Nikki hike back to Amsterdam, and Delia and Greg head to campus.

When they make it to the cabin, Nikki is breathing hard. *Thank God, the shrooms are wearing off*. They wait a while, but no teacher ever arrives. False alarm.

Gabriel sits on the couch. The fire's ash smolders, and a pale, late light comes through the window. "Technically, we're not doing anything wrong right now, Nik."

"No, we're not."

And perhaps because everything has been burned out of her, Nikki feels free. She lies on the couch with her head in Gabriel's lap. She lets him smooth her hair from her temples. The birds and crickets sound like a lullaby. Some tautness in her breaks, like scissors have snipped her marionette lines, and her limbs fall. She's collapsed, finally, into Gabriel. The way he touches her face is tender, and she can tell he wants to take care of her.

Nikki pulls his face to hers and kisses him. They kiss for

what seems like hours, her shirt off but bra on, bare back against the grimy sofa. Gabriel's weight is on her. She almost falls asleep in the amethyst dusk. He has to wake her, and they stand, groggy, and he picks a holly leaf from her tangled hair.

15

Delia's already worried about leaving Greg for Thanksgiving break. Maybe he can feel her clinging, because he's been pushing her away the past few days. Tonight they're sitting at dinner, and Josiah Sayden is talking about a field trip his American History class took to an old cemetery two towns over. He describes the plots, how the babies' graves were small and just had a single name. How the slaves were separated, and most of those stones were inscribed with no names.

No one looks at Greg when Josiah says the word *slaves*, but Delia feels like everyone wants to. She's staring at him, concerned, and doesn't even realize it until he looks at her and makes a face that says: "Quit staring."

Later, they're lying in the choir loft. Greg has an enormous bruise the color and shine of eggplant on his shin. She bends down to kiss it, but he pulls her away from his leg, with a bashful look—as though he's embarrassed to be coddled.

"But I'll make it better," she promises.

"No, don't," he says.

Somerset's doing a pre-Thanksgiving feed on this brisk November evening. Unlike other advisors who drop off pizza boxes in a dorm common room for their kids, Somerset has laid out sushi and tempura from the place in the next town, and is making miso soup. There's sparkling cider, lemonade, green tea.

Delia is the first to arrive. "Jesus, *Somerset*. Going all out here, aren't you?"

"You guys deserve a decent meal, I think."

"I'm not complaining, trust me."

"Where's your partner in crime?"

"Nikki? She's out to dinner, but she'll be sad she missed this."

Three timid Preps enter, one with glitter on her hands from art class. Delia wonders if she knows Parker. A tall lanky boy extends his hand to Somerset.

"Hello, Mr. Somerset. It is a pleasure to see you again."

Somerset smiles widely. "You too, James." He shakes James O'Rourke's hand firmly. "James, have you met

Delia? I believe you're both Californians."

Delia extends her hand. "Where you from in Cali, James?"

He looks at his starch-white New Balances. "Silicon Valley. Are you from L.A.?"

She smiles. "No, San Diego. Which means 'a whale's vagina' in German."

"No, it doesn't."

Delia's pleased that Somerset is laughing in the kitchen at her *Anchorman* reference. She nibbles on tempura and listens to Preps try to outdo one another with grades or accomplishments before announcing her escape. She misses Greg—as always. She wants to find him; she can't even relax here. "Okay, kids. Time for me to head."

Mr. Somerset follows her to the foyer. "Delia, what's been going on?" he asks, out of earshot of everyone.

She freezes, one arm halfway in her coat sleeve. *What has he heard?* "What are you talking about?" she says.

"What do you think? Algebra."

She looks down, relieved. She's been ignoring this problem, like someone who pretends her tooth doesn't hurt.

"Delia. We'll figure something out."

"Yeah, yeah," she says.

"Come talk to me Sunday morning, I'll introduce you to Mark Essing, he's a good tutor."

"Cool, thanks," she says. She shakes her head in the mauve evening. A squirrel knocks off the last few crackling leaves as it runs down a limb. Delia tells herself to stop being paranoid.

A couple days later, morning rain varnishes the school. Gabriel is taking Nikki to the Glendon Hotel brunch on this dark Sunday, to save their spirits. A few students lurk, but the majority are hiding in bed. It's just one of those days.

As they wait for their cab, he takes her hand, but after a minute, she pulls hers away.

"Nikki, I got to say this," he starts. "You, like . . ."

"What?" she says impatiently.

"You act, like, almost as if you don't want me near you sometimes." His hands are clutching the pockets of his Armani coat, and mud sticks to his Prada loafers. "It's like, you're very distant."

She feels terrible. She feels like they're assigned partners, and have been trying to make it work, but it's breaking down. Gabriel is cheerful, but it's finite—how far she can push him, or push him away.

"I'm sorry, Gabe. I swear it's me, not you. I just get lost in my thoughts."

Across the circle, Somerset's door opens.

"Hey, it's Delia," Gabriel says.

Delia slams the door. Her hair in a messy ponytail, rain boots over pajama bottoms.

"Whose place is that?" Gabriel asks.

"Our advisor."

"On a Sunday morning?"

"I don't know that she was doing anything wrong, Gabe."

"I didn't say she was!"

"Well, don't say that she is."

"Nik. Do I spread stuff? Am I that guy?"

"I just think that stupid rumors went around, and they shouldn't go around anymore."

"Is this my fault? You gotta stop being paranoid."

Nikki crosses her arms.

A few green-and-white faces represent Wellington's stab at school spirit. The fourteen million dollars the school spent for a *Friday Night Lights* look hasn't coaxed more fans to football games. There are no synchronized cheers or school flags, just wiseass, preppy guys talking trash to the opposing players.

Delia explains each running play. "I mean, why the hell would he call a draw play right after he just ran a trap?"

Nikki sighs with boredom. She hates being dragged to worship Greg.

"Are you even listening to me?"

Nikki rolls her eyes. "Have you noticed that it's twenty-seven to nothing? They're not coming back from this."

Delia gives Nikki the finger. Nikki grabs her arm and

leads her down the bleachers and back to their rooms for popcorn and gossip, *Teen Vogue* and Gwen Stefani.

Greg slouches in the game-room corner. Noah is replaying a stiff arm that Greg put on a poor 160-pound cornerback, which left the guy facedown on the field without his helmet.

"At least you fucked 'em up, Jenson. At least you fucked 'em up," Noah keeps saying.

Chase is next to Greg in the back corner, and for once they have located a common bitterness. Chase is hiding his mouth with his hand to dip.

Suddenly Greg whispers to Chase, and the guys stare sharply at Delia, who has just appeared from the student center. The look sends ice down her spine. *That was subtle.* Delia looks into Nikki's eyes, asking: *fight or flee?*

Nikki shakes her head, stunned by the wall of negative energy. Delia decides to move forward.

Greg looks away as she approaches the couch.

She slides onto the arm of the couch, but is careful not to touch him. "Hey, baby."

Greg doesn't respond, nor look in her direction.

So Delia grabs Greg's chin lightly and turns his head. "Hey. Why aren't you talking to me?" She gives him a playful sad face.

Greg knocks her hand away. "Not now."

Delia is floored, sits helpless. Nikki pulls her arm. "Let's go."

As Delia gets up, Chase furtively makes a gesture of knocking back a phantom bottle, to let her know what's happening.

As they walk away, Greg stands up.

"Thanks for waiting for me after the game, Deals. Thanks. That was *awesome*."

Chase tries to pull him down and shut him up; he's not slurring, but anyone can tell that he's not sober.

"I can explain, Greg," Delia says.

"The one game I really fuck up, and you don't want to be seen with me. I lost. You don't like it. Oh, I understand."

Chase wrangles him down, and Nikki shushes Delia. "You can't get through to him now," she keeps saying.

When the girls get into the hall, they look at each other, jaws dropped.

"*Shit,*" Delia says.

"He's been drinking. He can't drink."

"He's been drinking," Delia repeats, dazed. "Shit."

Nikki and Delia hole up in a quad by the chapel. Nikki talks her down for an hour. Greg's drunk, he's notorious for having tempers, and when he drinks, he's doubly dangerous. Nikki thinks Delia should wait till tomorrow to talk. But Delia doesn't want to sleep without talking to him.

"*Please* wait?" Nikki tries one more time.

Delia looks at her friend.

Nikki sighs. "Go find him, sweetie."

The fragrance is pungent as she opens the door to the observatory—Greg's Armani cologne, and Glenlivet. She tracked down Chase in his common room, and he directed her here. She feels her way through the pitch black, and she settles next to him where he's lying on the floor. His breathing is heavy.

Her eyes adjust, she can see shapes.

His jacket is folded underneath his head, and she makes out the outline of his white tank top as he sits to pull on a flask, which glitters in his hand.

What do I do? Delia feels helpless, stupid, unwanted. Part of her would like to share that flask. Part of her wants to get rid of it. She wants to kiss him, make him better that way. But she has no confidence. She's silent.

She feels Greg's eyes on her. They roll into each other, and he presses his hot face to her neck. When he bites her, she almost makes a loud noise but stifles herself.

He attempts to take off her shirt and it gets hopelessly tangled. He tries harder. When she starts to help him, he removes her fingers.

"Uh-uh. I got thisss," he slurs. Greg pins her hands over her head. "I got this."

His voice isn't harsh. He kisses her stomach.

Then he bites her stomach, harder. This is a weird game. And then she realizes all of a sudden that his face is wet. He's crying. She squirms, she doesn't know what to do. She feels him twisting the string on her thong and with a quick tug, he breaks it.

"No," she says. She gets up, stumbling, pulling her clothes together clumsily. Disoriented in the dark. "Why'd you do that? Greg, what's going on?" Her voice is unsteady, weak.

He sits on the floor, kneeling now, like a big child. He wipes his face. "Don't go."

But she's disquieted, her sense of balance so out of order she has to go find a lighted room to regain her bearings. She moves away from him, even as he reaches to console her.

16

Casey's waiting for Delia at the gate of the airport, her freckled shoulders shining. Her corn-blond hair has grown longer, almost touching the straps of her yellow sundress, and this throws Delia off—she didn't want anything to change while she was gone.

"Oh, my sweet petunia," Casey says as she grabs for her daughter. "God, I missed you, honey. I missed you too much."

Delia laughs, her voice muffled by her mom's embrace. "Oh my word, you're crushing me, Mom."

Delia smells her mother's fragrance, a combination of vanilla-bergamot hand cream and Dr. Bronner's soap and cinnamon Altoids. They pull apart, and look at each other, Casey holding Delia's free hand as Delia hefts her bag's strap higher on her shoulder. Casey squeezes her daughter's hand, and says it again: "I missed you too much."

Delia nods. She knows what her mother has just announced: *I'm sorry. I'm sorry you went away. You didn't need to go away.*

Driving with the top down in their old white Saab, Delia lets the California wind take her hair, and feels Wellington fall away. Palm trees, tall and straight, guard the coast. Seals loll on a cut of rock, some shiny black, others liverwurst-brown and crusted with salt, like oxidized metal.

Greg feels far away, and she's glad. He shook her up so bad her teeth are still rattling. The world seems wrong when he and she aren't right with each other.

Casey is chatting, driving erratically, nervous to have her daughter home. Casey talks over the Eagles on the radio, which is half static and she doesn't even notice. Delia leans forward, snaps off the music, and leans back, eyes closed.

"Turner and Mason are here, they're not at the house I don't think, but they're coming home to see you, they'll be home next half hour. And Will is arriving tomorrow morning, and bringing Kala."

"Mnnh," Delia says drowsily.

"And your father may or may not be showing up around four tomorrow."

Casey says this in a trimmed tone.

"What are you talking about? He e-mailed me he would definitely be here."

"I know, honey."

"*Well?* I mean, *largely* why I came home was to see him," Delia says meanly.

Casey looks at her daughter, and takes a left up their drive. Angel's Trumpet flowers hang dolefully from vines on the fence. A cat slinks away from the front door, where it was basking in the sun. Casey apologizes but offers no explanation.

"Did you guys fight about something stupid, is that why he's not coming?"

They're getting Delia's bag out of the trunk now, and Casey's shaking her head. The family made an agreement last year, after too much gossip was slung like mud around the precious rooms of the house, that stuff between Sam and Casey would be kept private.

Delia growls like a dog now, out of sheer frustration.

In her room, she feels like Alice in Wonderland after she ate the tea cake that made her grow. Why had she never noticed how tiny this attic room is? Tattered posters Scotch-taped to the wall, of Laird and Slater and the Hawaii Women's Surf Team. Soccer trophies on the shelf, along with family pictures and beads, seashells, a rubber dolphin bath toy.

She looks out the window. The view stretches down the

golden world. She presses her nose against the screen, breathing in California. To think of Glendon now is to remember a snow globe, cheap and unreal, shaken so the place is obscured by whiteness.

Turner and Mason. Only one year apart, twenty and nineteen, and they're more like twins. And both of them are the baby brothers to the indomitable and strong-jawed Will, so they're allies as well. Delia sits on the couch with them, fighting over the remote because it makes them feel like they live here and are nowhere close to growing up, instead of spread across the country, and step-by-reluctant-and-exhilarated-step leaving home and childhood.

Turner's got it now, and holds it out of reach. It's Animal Planet, and they're showing surgery of a cat. The animal is gassed, its stomach slit.

"Gross, Turn, come on, change it," Delia yells, grinning and pouting.

"This is foul, dude," Mason says, arms folded.

Outside the screen door, in the violet shade of the star jasmine, their own cats sit and peer inside with luminous eyes, attentive to some emergency.

"Check that little guy out, shit, look at his blissed-out smile, man. He has no *idea* what the hell's going on," Turner says gleefully to the TV.

"Okay, let's get out of here. Who wants to get burgers?

Maybe catch a flick at Roserum?" Mason asks.

Turner pushes Delia off the couch. "Go see what Mom's planning tonight. She probably wants us out of here, anyway."

"Why don't *you* go ask?" Delia says, but she's already sullenly walking up the stairs, accustomed and even flattered after all these years to being bossed around by her brothers.

The upstairs hall windows are open, and the sheer, white curtains are blowing out and being sucked in. She can hear the murmur of her mother's voice coming from the linen room, and heads that way. A cat jumps from a bookcase, and its calico body blurs down the rug. Delia is about to say "Mom" to let her know she's there but then she hears something.

"I know, Sammy," Casey says. "I'm well aware of what I said. But I changed my mind."

Delia stops breathing.

"God, Sam, I *know*! But I don't mind if you bring her, if that means you'll come. I just want you to be here. The kids are looking forward to a great night. Bring her. I don't care."

Delia feels sick.

"I'm *being* honest. I don't mind at all. Bring her." And then she says with forced good cheer: "Come on, I've got turkey, fresh cranberry chutney, andouille stuffing, you name it. We'll have a good time."

Delia walks backward, as if by doing so, instead of turning around and walking away, she can undo what she just heard.

When she gets downstairs, her brothers look at her.

"What's up, sis?" Turner asks.

"Why don't we make Mom dinner, just like spaghetti and stuff," Delia says as casually as possible. "I mean, she's going to be cooking all day tomorrow."

"*You* make it," Mason says.

"Screw you," Delia says, kicking one of her flip-flops at him.

He shields his face, laughing. "Easy, tiger. Damn, she got a temper."

But they all end up in the kitchen, playing Allman Brothers on the old stereo, sautéing onions, drinking Heineken, singing along: "*Walk along the river, sweet lullaby, it just keeps on flowing, it don't worry 'bout whe-e-e-re it's going,* no, *no.*"

After dinner, Delia and the boys throw a Frisbee around the yard in the porch light, but they hit one another in the head or send the ring into the thickets.

"I can't see shit out here," Mason complains happily.

Delia notices her mom collecting her reading glasses and book, looking around the kitchen to make sure everything is off, displaying the usual signs of heading to bed. Delia lets her brothers keep playing and she steps into the house. Casey looks at her daughter.

"Do you need something, honey?" Casey asks.

Delia clumsily walks up to her, but stops short of hugging her. Instead she plays with the whisk in the utensil jar. "I missed you," she says, looking at the floor.

Casey kisses her daughter on the forehead, and Delia is too shy to look into her eyes.

She lies in bed, looking at a seashell night-light that's been steadfastly burning since she was little. Some nights you hear the ocean, but not tonight. Delia hears one word: *Greg.* It leaves a tracer in her head.

He owes *her* a call. His drinking got them fighting, it should be his apology. But every minute that goes by now gets bloodier, the rip harder to mend, and sleep less likely. As mad as she is, it's worse to imagine losing him.

Finally her phone rings. The photo she took in the lake house bed, his back stark against the sheets, comes up on the small screen.

"Hi-i-i-i," she says.

"Hey, Deals," he says without confidence.

She sits up. "Yes?"

He clears his throat. Tries to laugh. "I just *cannot* drink."

She waits a beat. "No, you sure can't."

"I wasn't really angry that you left the game. I was just fucked up."

"Gotcha," she says.

"Baby, I'm so sorry," he says now in a low voice. "I love you."

And that's all it takes. They gain momentum till they're purring. She tells him she found a stem of bougainvillea growing up through a rusted hole in the MG's floor. He says it's hailing in Brooklyn. They talk until they sleep.

The birds are jacked up for a storm, the cats are skittish, but the sky isn't dark enough to mean rain. Delia rambles around the yard, too old to play on the wooden jungle gym, and too restless to sit around. She touches leaves and petals to make sure they're real, but her face is impassive.

It's 3:45, he should be here any moment. With "her." There have been a long string of "her"s, some real, visible, even beautiful, most of them young, a number of them pre-divorce and double that ever since, and a few of them mythological—sometimes the kids only suspected there was a her because of his absence, his absent-mindedness, his strong-jawed, deep-voiced, radiant happiness.

Mason plops down in the grass next to Delia. "What's the word, kid?" he asks.

"Kid," Delia mutters. "You're more immature than me."

"What?!" he protests, running his hands over the grass absentmindedly.

"I heard you making dive-bombing noises while you

ate your granola this morning."

He laughs, then sighs. Looks at the sky. Delia realizes he's waiting for their dad too, waiting to see if he comes, if he comes with *her*, or if he comes too late for it to matter. Mason might not even know that's why he's out here, but it is.

And then the gray BMW rolls up the drive. Brother and sister squint at the window, unable to pick out silhouettes. The driver's door opens. Sam steps out in a jacket, a half case of wine under his arm, his chestnut hair mussed. The kids wait. Sam pivots and sees them, and he gives a salute, then smiles. They wait for the other door to open.

It doesn't. He's alone.

Delia gets up, trembling with gratitude. "Hey," she greets him, playing it cool.

"Hey, baby," he says happily. "How's my girl?"

Inside, apple cider simmers with cloves and cinnamon and nutmeg on the iron stove, the turkey is mahogany-skinned inside the oven, there's cranberry-ginger relish, paprika-creamed spinach. Casey toasted Parmesan crisps and everyone pops those into their mouths, as well as olives, and salmon on black bread. Delia is allowed champagne, although Casey twice tells her to slow down when she catches her refilling her glass.

"Mom, this smells incredible," Turner says again, trying the relish with his pinkie.

"Thank you, thank you," Casey says, her cheeks pink

from the champagne, the kitchen heat, and the attention.

"I'm banking on the creamed spinach," Sam says benevolently, at home in his old house.

"Seriously," Mason agrees. "I get high on that stuff."

"You do, don't you?" Delia says as if he's a freak, and they all laugh.

No one notices the dilapidated airport cab squeaking to a stop under the trellis of Easter lily vine. Or Will helping Kala from the backseat, the silk pleats of her turquoise dress shining against the old pleather of the car seat. Her face, like an Asian mask, is ethereal. Will handles their luggage as if it was weightless, and they walk to the front door. They even get inside before the loud kitchen party sees them.

"You guys are sneaky!" Casey squeals as she takes off her apron to properly hug them.

There's hugs and kisses, and greetings and barbs. But Will and Kala are strangely still and beatific. Their quiet makes everyone uneasy, and talk drops off. Delia looks at the yin and yang couple: Will, with his sun-weathered face, burned hair, his frame—broken and healed in years of surfing and climbing and mountain biking, and Kala, her creamy face unscarred, her bones whole and straight, her supernatural calm.

Their postures are even opposite, and their hands, his so clumsy and wide and marked, and hers so deft and lovely and—

"Oh my God," Delia says.

She's the first to see the diamond. It's all Will could afford on his salary, but it lights the room like a star.

"Ho-ly *shit*," Turner says.

Casey clutches at Kala. Sam looks at his firstborn, and he and Mason, without meaning to, say in unison: "You son of a bitch."

This is how the Bretons congratulate the couple on being engaged.

After dinner, they light the outdoor fireplace, sit on canvas chairs, drink red wine, and laugh about the past, the present, and the future. Avoiding the glaciers of bad memories that could sink the ship of good feeling. Mason is downright drunk, and he keeps starting a story about a girl named Jill, and then he forgets the rest.

Casey and Sam sit together. His shirt unbuttoned, slacks wrinkled, his body easy. And Casey sits in good yoga form, her face perched like a cat's on her neck. Her eyes take in everything, sparkling with flame.

Mason and Turner argue about who will be Will's best man.

"Dude, you're the one that totaled Will's Jetta the day after he got it," Turner accuses his brother.

"Oh, wait, I'm sorry," Mason slurs sarcastically. "Who used Will's credit card in Tijuana for those goddamn

Oxycodones, huh?"

Will looks up from drawing circles in the dirt with a twig. "I never knew about that one, to be honest."

Mason cups his mouth with his hand, and Sam laughs.

"Who's your best woman?" Delia asks Kala.

Everyone laughs, except Kala. "You mean maid of honor?" she says.

Delia shrugs, mortified.

"You are," Kala says. "I hope. I don't have a sister."

Delia turns away, even as she nods, to hide childish pride. And jealousy.

She's so happy for them, and so sad.

It's the same confusion when she wakes up the next morning. It rained in the night, and the leaves and blossoms are heavy. Mist sits over the yard. And there in the drive, its windshield beaded, is the BMW.

"Jesus," Delia says aloud to herself.

And she thinks: *Is this joy or terror?*

She tiptoes down the hall to check the guest room. The door is wide open. On the perfectly made, unslept-in bed two cats are coiled around each other. The Siamese lifts its chin, glares with its sky-blue marbles, makes it clear she is unwanted on this threshold.

The weather never breaks, but on Saturday the guys decide they have to get one surf in before they go separate ways.

Kala and Delia languish on the beach. Delia could surf, but the riptides this time of year are frightening; they make her believe in God.

Kala's billowing skirt catches the breeze and blows up, and she laughs, hauls it down like a sail. Delia's in jeans and a big sweatshirt. Lumps of damp seaweed lie on the hard flat sand. The boys shimmer out there in black wet suits.

"Let's walk," Kala says, standing and offering a hand.

They stroll, slow and zigzagging, down the mostly empty beach. A guy throws a tennis ball into the waves for his Lab. Kala talks about her job at the bank, haltingly, then more candidly. She hates it, doesn't feel like she belongs. Delia realizes that Kala is confiding in her. She starts paying attention, making compassionate statements.

"You *think*?" Kala asks, wrinkling her nose. It's her trademark statement.

"Completely," Delia says, her own trademark statement, the one she throws out to people even when she's not sure about anything, except that she loves them.

The bluffs shiver, and birds caw and shriek, and Delia gets dizzy as she watches the surf surge and then crash, and start over.

In the distance, two girls are walking a Great Dane. Delia stops, looks.

"Why don't we head back?" she says to Kala.

But not even this could taint her day. She knows who

that was: Celeste and her friend Karina. She half listens to Kala on the way back, and half wonders why Seth never told Nikki the reason Celeste wasn't allowed to hang out with Delia Breton ever again.

17

After the fourth episode in a row, Nikki has finally had enough of the *Real World* marathon and of her childhood bedroom. *This is pathetic. What am I doing here?*

Plainview is gray and deathly boring this week. The nightly basement parties with beer pong and whippets are redundant, and it doesn't help that Vanessa officially has a new best friend: Renee Koplawski. Who lives alone with her mother, and her mother spends half her week in New Jersey with her new boyfriend, so there's an empty house at the girls' fingertips. Nikki was there yesterday, while the girls made popcorn and ate Vicodin and watched snowboard videos, rating the guys. Renee and Ness also made sure to mention every fun thing that happened all fall, using nicknames and code words, and laughing at odd moments, to be certain that Nikki knew her place: outside the ring.

You put yourself there, Ness's face communicated sometimes when she looked at Nikki as Renee chatted on and on, her voice mellow with pills. Nikki couldn't breathe. She faked a call from her dad telling her to come home, and walked through Plainview. Her breath steamed. She took Abalont Drive to Geary Lane to Cherry Road, past guys working on Japanese motorbikes in driveways, past cheap houses with ornate columns, through a crowd of Rollerblading girls in Little Princess sweatshirts who gave Nikki the finger when she didn't get out of their way.

Where am I?

Now there's a knock on her bedroom door. Rocco, the rottweiler, who's curled on her bed with her, barks.

"Entrez," Nikki shouts.

Sharon peeks around the door, still in yoga pants and a green tank with NAMASTE GIRL scripted in white across her breasts.

"Hey, Nik. I'm heading to the Saks outlet. You want to come?" Sharon stands just inside Nikki's bedroom, cracking her Orbit.

"Can't. I'm busy." Nikki gives a lopsided grin.

"Come *on,* a little retail-therapy will lift your spirits."

Geez, even Sharon senses something's wrong with me. "Really, no thanks, I'm fine."

"Well, if you change your mind, just let me know, okay?"

Nikki gets a call from Delia. They talk every day, commiserating about long-distance boyfriends.

"Why don't *you* go visit Greg? Can't you take the train to the city?" Delia asks.

"I don't know if he would want me to."

"He'd be psyched. Plus, you could let me know what he's like in his element."

"Sugar, I don't know. He's your boyfriend."

"He was your friend before he was my boyfriend. I don't own him."

Nikki chews on the idea. *Does Delia really want me to go see Greg or is this a challenge?* She feels shy but calls.

"What's up, cuz?" she says.

"Hey, girl," he answers. "Didn't expect to hear from you."

"I'm *bored*," she groans.

"I know what you're saying. What's the story?"

"Can I come in and play tomorrow?" she asks in a little girl voice.

He hesitates. "Yeah, a'ight. Um, I'm going to see *Alien* tomorrow with one of my friends, but it's cool if you roll too."

"Excellent. Random, but excellent."

"It's part of this festival." He pauses, then speaks away

from the phone. "Yeah, Ma. I will. I will, two seconds." Then he says, "We got dinner cookin', here."

"What are you having?" she asks.

"Curry something. The usual grub, man."

"Yum," Nikki says. "Save some for me."

"Well, Nikki hits Brooklyn. This should be good. I gotta run, I'll e-mail you where to meet up and shit. Cool?"

"Cool," she says.

She lies back on her bed. Suburbia chirps and beeps outside her window. Madonna the dog pokes into the room, sees Rocco, and turns up her nose and leaves. Nikki thinks about Greg's universe, his mother's island accent drifting through narrow halls, the smell of curry stew reaching his bedroom. His single bed, the slanted ceiling tacked with football heroes, his ceiling light in a basketball shape. Nikki feels nervous, as if she'd never talked to him before and this was a blind date.

Her father doesn't put up an argument when she asks if she can take the train in tomorrow. He's got his big feet in black socks propped by the fire, listening to Josh Groban. Madonna glares at Nikki from his lap, where she finally found solace.

"Brooklyn." Vic sighs. "My roots, sweetie. Fort Greene isn't Bensonhurst, but they got a lot to do with each other. You know, we should go in more often. I got a lot of places where you need to eat, old places you need to witness, princess, before they tear them down."

"I'm in." Nikki shrugs.

"Tell Greg hi from me, yeah?" It was no secret that Greg impressed him the most out of any of her friends. "And be home before seven. Be home for dinner."

Nikki's train car is empty except for a middle-aged couple blabbing on cell phones. A swastika is carved into the metal window frame. Nikki cranks Stephen Marley on her iPod; this becomes a soundtrack to the frost-stripped trees, the junkyards, and generators that blur by. She puts her knees against the seat in front of her, and drifts off.

The train arrives at Atlantic Avenue, gliding and clacking into the long tunnel. It's culture shock to leave the dead lawns and big houses of Plainview for this underground of lights and oily track and people moving in every direction. She finds a stairway up and makes her way through bitter wind to the Starbucks where they're meeting. She can see Greg through the glass window and taps, and he looks around with a slow smile and a nod. A gaunt, tall black girl with an oval face sits with him. This isn't the "friend" she'd been expecting.

Nikki walks inside apprehensively.

"Hey, Greg." Nikki hovers over them.

"Nik, what's up?" Greg stands and gives Nikki a hug. "This is Erica."

The tall girl smiles but doesn't get up. Her eyes are gray and sad and beautiful. "What's up?"

"Oh, hey. Nice to meet you." Nikki sticks out her hand and they shake. "Sorry, my hands are freezing."

Erica gives Nikki that disarming, almost disinterested smile again.

"Erica and I been friends since we were four," Greg says.

"Oh yeah? Cool."

"Don't worry. I won't ruin y'alls' hot date," Erica says.

"Oh, God, that's not what this is," Nikki hurries to say. "His girlfriend is my best friend."

Erica widens her eyes at Greg. "Oh, really," she says slowly.

Greg gets his wallet out. "Nik, you want some sort of ten-dollar coffee before we roll?"

"That's okay. I'm saving up for popcorn."

"All right then, let's split." Greg stands and pulls on a puffy black down parka with a huge fur collar.

"Nice fur." Nikki strokes the collar. "Kitty-kat?" Greg never wears this coat at Wellington.

"You preppy chicks into PETA or something?" Erica stands and pulls on her army fatigue jacket, which also has a fur collar.

Nikki blushes with embarrassment. *Did she really just call me preppy?*

The air bites. Nikki buttons up her collar and adjusts her

scarf. They pass town houses, some of which lean toward their neighbors, their stoops hedged by iron railings. A ratty, stained poodle scratches at the window of a first-floor apartment as they go by. Two kids sit on one stoop, even in the cold, their backpacks on the steps, playing PS3s.

The Brooklyn Academy of Music takes up an entire block. Greg tells her how it was built when this area of Brooklyn was home to the "white fat cats."

"You must come here a lot." Nikki looks up at the columns. Twenty-foot banners promoting the Fall Gala hang down to the sidewalk. The building is obviously more than a movie theater. She's never been anywhere like this.

"Used to. Erica was in a dance group that performed here a bunch."

"That's awesome. You still dance?" Nikki looks over to her.

"Sometimes," she says, and although Nikki waits for more, that's all she gets.

At the ticket window Nikki offers to pay for their tickets, and Greg shoots her a look.

"My dad gave me some money," Nikki tries to explain. "He said I should treat." *Great, now I sound like a spoiled brat.*

"We need to go Dutch." Greg comes to the rescue. "Keep this shit platonic."

The inside of the theater reverberates with decades of performance. Its stage, red curtains, and chandelier give her the shivers. The matinee is pretty empty so they find seats quickly. Nikki is relieved when the lights dim.

"That movie scared the effing *crap* out of me," Nikki says outside on the front steps. It's gotten dark but is only a little after four.

"Hell yeah, it did. You practically ripped my arm off." Greg smiles.

"Sorry. But that's what you get for taking me."

"It was worth it." Greg buttons up his parka. "Shit was pretty hot on the big screen."

"You know, Delia would love that flick. She loves that type of action. You should watch it with her."

"Who's Delia?" Erica interrupts.

"That's my friend from school," Greg answers quickly.

"Is he the ghetto superstar up there?" Erica asks Nikki. "I bet he is."

"He's definitely a star," Nikki says, certain that there's no right answer.

"All right, y'all, I'm out," Erica says, walking backward in the other direction now. "I've got a few friends too, you know? Good to meet you, Nikki."

"Great to meet you too."

Since Nikki has time to kill, Greg shows her Fort Greene. They walk past brownstones, rows of trees towering, and

Greg points out Spike Lee's house. They pass Greg's sushi place, lit up with a white lantern. They go by Frank's, the best bar in the five boroughs.

"They play old school R and B there and shit. They have the best jukebox ever, full of, like, Sam Cooke and Stevie Wonder and Bessie Smith. These old guys, they come out in their purple fedoras, and their three-piece suits, you know? They get their Hennessy and Coke. The ladies all come in, play cards in the back room. Sundays, they got a buffet with collards and mac-and-cheese and fried chicken, all the good shit."

But Nikki isn't paying him full attention. "Have you spoken with Delia?" Nikki finally asks.

"Today? I've been with you all day." He pops a cough drop in his mouth.

"No, I mean, just over break."

"Yeah, I talk to her almost every day. She's been hanging with her brothers and their friends," he answers as if it's a silly question.

They're silent, walking past a piano school, notes drifting out of the top-story window.

"Would Erica like her?" Nikki asks.

"What are you getting at, Nik?" His voice is slightly cold.

"Nothing. Nothing."

He turns then and stops. "Erica and I are friends, and

that's it. We been friends my whole life. You got it?"

"Easy," Nikki says. "She just didn't know who Delia is."

He rolls his eyes, exhales with frustration. They proceed in silence. They've come to a park. They climb to an empty picnic table that overlooks empty tennis courts. A man pushing a shopping cart of cans rattles down the hill, talking to no one and seeming to have a pleasant conversation. Two girls lean into each other by a tree to light a cigarette, one cupping her hands for the other.

"Let's just say," Greg says quietly, "that I didn't *feel* like telling Erica that I'm seeing a white girl." Then he looks at Nikki with those big eyes, black as ebony, and challenging.

"Whoa. Sorry, I guess this isn't my territory."

He puts his hands in his pockets, looks out at his hometown. "It's cool. Let's just not talk about it again."

They sit, shivering. A dog-walker comes by with five dogs straining at separate leashes. A caramel-beige pit bull with black lips leads the pack.

Finally Nikki speaks up. "It must be tough having a dog in the city. I mean, this is as good as it gets for them."

"As good as it gets?" Greg says testily.

Nikki looks at him in alarm, but then he laughs.

"I'm messing with you, girl."

"Damn!" Nikki laughs. "Don't do that! I thought I was in trouble again."

"Naw. You ain't in trouble. I hope I'm not either." He

looks at her sideways then.

"Greg. Delia is *crazy* about you."

He smiles like a kid and tries to hide it by turning his face. "Yeah, yeah, yeah. Whatever."

"She is."

"Well, she's it, you know. She's it for me."

Nikki nods, unable to speak, sort of breathless.

18

Nikki and Delia hug and jump around when they see each other. But the joy doesn't last. The time between Thanksgiving and Christmas break isn't long, and yet it's forever. Everyone straps on their boots.

Nikki misses Seth more than ever. She tries to write a paper, but clicks her inbox a thousand times. She surfs iTunes for sugary, sickening songs about love. She ate two cheeseburgers yesterday, and could have eaten two more. When she went to sleep last night she fell into an indigo quagmire of anxiety before she finally sat up and read by flashlight; anything to keep her mind out of the dark swamp.

Then she saw the pictures.

Nikki and Delia are hanging out in Delia's room, trading

stories and trying on clothes. Nikki's looking through Delia's digital camera pictures and she sees Seth at a house party.

"You saw him?" Nikki asks now.

"Yeah, he sends his love. I thought I told you that. He looks good. He looks like a guy from New York."

He looks like he's on top of the world. Friends have their arms around his shoulders. Everyone's face is greasy and golden in the flash, and grinning. In another picture is a tall blond girl wearing Seth's windbreaker.

"Who's that?" Nikki asks.

"No one," Delia says, looking over Nikki's shoulder. "No one I know."

"She must have come with him," Nikki accuses Delia.

"I don't think she did. Honestly."

"She's wearing his windbreaker."

Is this why Seth doesn't want her to visit him at school? She can't put down the camera; she's caught between wanting to lick his picture and stick pins in the girl. They have big plans for Christmas break, when he'll stay with her family in Plainview. But that's too many calendar pages away. And he's way too effing happy. He never mentioned Gabriel after that one call, and Nikki was relieved. But now she's sure he isn't worried because he doesn't care.

"Why doesn't he just come to Glendon for the weekend?" Delia asks.

"I've asked," Nikki answers glumly. "He will not come

near this place. He'd probably burn it down if he did."

Delia plays with the camera. She points it at Nikki: *"Une, deux, trois."* Nikki blinks at the flash. Delia looks at the shot: this sad, voluptuous face, brown hair glossy to the shoulders, the gold chains winking. "Okay," Delia continues. "I double-dog dare you to ask Somerset if you can go off campus to New York."

"Are you crazy?" Nikki asks, grinning.

Delia shrugs, takes another picture, and this time Nikki does her Dita Von Teese for the photograph. "In case you didn't notice, he has a crush on us," Delia assures her. "He'll let you do what you want. You just have to *ask* him right."

"No way."

"Way."

The English and History Wing is thick with tradition. The wood paneled walls are oily with decades of life. The offices are a warren of bow-tie aristocrats with posters of the Black Panthers, and Harvard PhDs retranslating *The Iliad*, and desks are stacked with papers and books on everything from *The Andy Warhol Diaries* to the Franco-Prussian War.

"Nik, to what do I owe the pleasure?" Somerset spins in his chair.

Nikki sits next to him. "Nothing. Just coming over to say hi to my favorite young teacher."

"Your favorite, huh? You realize I have never taught you, right?"

"That's not why, silly. You look out for us. I just wanted to see what you've been up to." She smiles, realizes she's shaking.

Somerset rubs his eyes and sighs. "What's wrong, Nicole?" he says quietly.

She baby-pouts. "I want to go to New York this weekend."

Somerset leans back. "Okay-y-y."

"Can I?"

Now he laughs uncomfortably. "I don't know, can you?"

She looks blankly at him.

"We have this little thing called the sign-out system, Nik, I think you're acquainted with it," Somerset says. "You know, your sign-out form, the one your parent signs?"

"Ugh, Somerset!" she cries. "My father is out of the *country*, there's no *way* I'll get in touch with him."

"Well, maybe you should try," he says gently.

Nicole wipes "tears" from her eyes. "Isn't there another way?"

"There's no other way."

Nikki moves her hand close to his, so that she can feel warmth. He briskly pulls his away and stands. She stands too, shocked, embarrassed.

She tries to laugh. "Jesus. I'm a mess, huh? And I'm about to miss dinner. Just forget all this, it was stupid. I don't need to go anywhere."

Somerset is standing defensively in the corner. "I'm sorry I couldn't help," he blusters. "You're always welcome to chat, Nikki. None of us has all the answers, but we try."

She's already out the door.

When she finds Delia in the dining hall, spooning meatballs out of a steaming metal tray, she hisses in her ear: "Worst idea ever."

Delia turns, licks spaghetti sauce from her finger as Nikki walks away. "Whoops," she tries to say with humor.

The week just gets worse. Winter forces life inside. Everyone feels like they're living in a root cellar. The dorm, in particular, turns on itself. Girls lie around and play with their belly rings, eat jelly donuts, letting the jam spill and not caring. Hair plugs the shower drains.

Disorders bloom like hothouse flowers. The anorexic girls slice their apples thinner and thinner. The girls who throw up bring their terrible art to a peak, mastering silence, discretion, immediacy. The cutters take out their kits, hidden in Polo sunglass cases and blue velvet jewelry boxes. Someone even pens Columbine daydreams in her diary.

Keisha, who plays Southern rap too loud whenever she wants, seems to do it because the girls won't ask her to stop. She taunts them. But the rest of the girls, like little white maids in a castle, are afraid of "what it would mean" to ask the black girl on the floor to lower her Lil Wayne.

The only funny thing is when Olivia gets a piñata in the mail from her dad for her birthday. The girls string it up, in its Technicolor, Mexican glory, from a branch of the Japanese maple on Saturday afternoon. It snowed the night before, and when Olivia, blindfolded with a scarf, bats the container in half, candy and toy trinkets fly out into the snow. The girls become children, pawing the white ground, laughing, pushing one another.

But the next week starts off wrong again. The soccer field is dark with cold. Delia, in taking a brutal shot at the goal, gets Kerri in the face with the hard ball. Kerri has to sit down, and Coach Margonson hurries over with a water bottle. Kerri's nose is bleeding.

"Save that for the enemy," the coach says, looking back at Delia.

Delia's ashamed.

Nikki sits in the snack bar with Gabriel. She dips her second grilled cheese into ketchup and looks at him without listening. She just pulled an all-nighter to finish a poli sci paper, and she watches his matinee idol mouth and just doesn't give a rat's ass.

Delia, to put the cherry on top, fails another algebra quiz. She spins open her mailbox to find Somerset's green note.

Delia detects a whisper of tobacco in the dark history offices. She finds it amusing that Wellington teachers go to such lengths to catch students breaking rules, but are too lazy to smoke outside themselves. When she opens Somerset's door, the culprit is obvious.

"It's bad for your health," she tells him with a straight face.

"I'm glad you care," he says.

"Okay. What did I do now?"

Somerset holds up the quiz, 67 circled in red ink.

"Look, Delia, you're on the verge of failing. Upper-form year, colleges are going over your transcript with a microscope. You *gotta* pass. Do you understand?"

She nods. "Mr. Somerset, I'm *trying*. I meet with Mark, he's tutoring me twice a week."

Somerset's craggy face is sad and indecisive.

"What?" Delia prods.

"Nothing, it's just. I don't know."

"*What?*"

"Delia, look. You're tied up in a lot of things that are, how shall I say, unacademic."

"*What?* I work my butt off to get everything done."

He's flustered. "You might take time for yourself."

"What are you talking about?"

"Listen, you and Greg are very . . . public, and some faculty have wondered how *either* of you get your work done."

208

He smiles to soften the blow.

She stares him down. "Is this because we're, like, a mixed couple?"

Somerset sighs. "Delia, that has absolutely nothing to do with this."

"I think it does."

"Your choice to think that. But for the record, you're the one bringing that into this, no one else is."

Delia trawls the library, storming up the stairs. She wants to find Greg and complain about math, life, snow. Whatever. She can lose herself in him.

The library's bustling. IMs ping across the world. Politics-geeks scour periodicals, jocks luxuriate in the sports page, a row of faces are lit blue in front of the main computers.

Greg's is the only voice she can hear up the stairwell. *You have got to be kidding me.* His arms are wrapped around a Prep. Delia watches as they mock wrestle until he looks up.

"Oh shit. What's up, baby? Thought you had class right now." Greg grins broadly.

Delia stares at the Prep, who's still giggling. Their eyes lock and the girl lowers her head, sneaks a look at Greg, and excuses herself.

"All right. I'll see you later on, Patricia." Greg nods, and then looks back at Delia. "So what's up, baby? You came to find me?" He wraps his hands around her waist and kisses her neck. "I got all day free."

Delia pushes him away. "What were you doing with her?"

"Who? Patricia?"

"No, the *other* girl I found you groping, asshole."

Greg sighs deeply. "Delia, don't start shit, please. We were *playing*. Before you got up here there was a whole crew of us. Now, chill." Greg reaches, but she backs away.

"I'm serious, Greg. You would lose your mind if I did that."

"If you were hanging out with a cute Prep girl?"

"Oh, shut up."

"I wasn't doing shit, *all right*? I'm not going to tell you again. I'm sick of drama. Now come here." Greg pulls Delia closer to him.

"Whatever you say, Greg." She backs away. "Sometimes I wonder if you can be trusted."

"Me?" he screeches, and laughs bitterly, his hands pointing to his chest. "You're the one with a reputation."

Her blood gets cold. "What did you say?"

"I think you heard me."

Delia slowly turns on her heel and tries to make it to the stairs without fainting.

"Where you going?" he calls after her.

"None of your business."

"Where you *going*?"

Delia shakes her head as she descends. *Where am I going, good question.*

The Submarines croon out of Bose speakers in Delia's room. Delia's bent over her algebra work sheets at her desk, and Nikki's lying against a beanbag and highlighting her psych textbook.

"I can't believe he was with her," Nikki says again after a silent spell. "This week, everything's just gone to shit. Completely to *shit*."

"Oh yeah. It has. I can barely see my way out of this work. I mean, I finish one thing, I have three other things that are now late."

Nikki closes her book. "I feel kind of manic, you know? I *need* to see Seth, but no one's giving us a pass to the city. My parents wouldn't even think of it."

"Tell them you're going on a college visit to NYU. I'm so *sure* they'll buy it," Delia smirks.

"Please, *your* parents are going to give you permission? Aren't you failing math?"

"The whole sign-out thing is retarded. They act like we can't take care of ourselves, like we're in third grade." Delia caps her pen. She looks out her window at sunset: blood red shining through the black tangle of trees. "You know, I just thought of something."

Nikki shivers at Delia's smile. "Uh-oh."

"My friend Charlie works at my dad's office."

Nikki waits to understand.

"He could fax the permission slip from my dad's office, so it comes from the number in the school's file. He could call in to make sure they received it, and say he's my dad. That we're meeting him in New York this weekend because he's going to be there on business."

"Oh God, that's crazy."

"It's a little crazy," Delia agrees.

"Somerset has to sign off too. My dad has to sign off."

"Charlie will call your dad."

Nikki thinks. "If we get busted, we're screwed."

"If we get signed out, we're going to have so much fun."

Nikki smiles nervously at Delia. "I can't believe we're going to do this."

Delia leaves a message on Charlie's cell phone. When she clicks off, the girls shake their heads, amazed at their own balls.

A thud on the dark glass.

They both jump. "What the hell was that?" Nikki asks.

"I bet it was a bird."

They run out of the building without jackets. They take a stick and push around the azalea bushes near the building. The leaves are curled up and splotchy. The sun is vanished, and the girls shake. Then they see the grackle, in the light from the windows of the building. On his back, claws up, dead as a doornail.

"Shit," Nikki says under her breath. "Is this an omen?"

Delia looks at her.

The stunned grackle rustles together his wings, and turns over in a clumsy, self-conscious hurry, like a drunk man realizing he'd fallen asleep in the road. His golden eyes glisten as he looks this way and that in panic. Then he flaps his wings and flies into the sky, the black of his feathers merging with the black of the night.

"Yeah, it's an omen," Delia says. "A good omen. He can fly, he's alive."

19

Delia refuses to wear long johns under her soccer shorts, and the wind bites. Her vision blurs as cold air burns her eyes. Wellington is playing Kent, who they usually beat. It's a team of wan, bedraggled blond girls. But this year they have number 43, easily six feet, black hair plaited in a french braid down her neck, with legs that can take her from one end zone to the other in three strides. She looks Native American or Pakistani, Delia isn't sure. The girl rules the field, and it looks like she's going to score again.

"Go, Deals, get her!" Nikki shouts hoarsely. She's jumping on the sidelines in her white jeans, North Face jacket, Gucci glasses. Breath steaming.

Delia pounds the turf after 43, knowing she can't catch

up, but at least if a defender sends her sideways, Delia will be there.

There's four minutes left, and she struggles to forget that Nikki's got their duffels, that a cab from Glendon Taxi is waiting in the hockey rink lot. Every time she thinks about it, her heart does a broken-beat drum-and-bass solo, and she nearly bites the lawn.

Nikki's not just overexcited about the game, she's worried they'll miss their train. And terrified that someone will call them on their false sign-out.

Number 43 skitters like a horse; Delia feels like a plodding dog nipping at her heels. Then 43 kicks, scores. The last forty seconds of the game are stupid. Kent gets the ball, and they play with it, keeping it away from the other team till the end horn.

Delia does the mandatory handshaking, has a quick exchange with her coach, and nabs a water bottle. She and Nikki run-walk up the hill, guilty as sin, euphoric.

The girls slide into the taxi. Delia's legs are chafed, red, scratched, her face ruddy. Nikki's shivering.

"Jailbreak," Nikki whispers.

"Dude, I'm filthy. I can't believe I didn't get to take a shower."

But the girls are still grinning. Nikki looks at the time on her phone. "Shit, we've got like twelve minutes."

"Uh-oh."

"Hey, mister," Nikki says, sliding her arms over the passenger seat in front of her. "We've *got* to get that train, we're dying to get into the city. Any way you can kind of step on the gas?"

The guy is burly, and he turns his head like an owl to look at Nikki. Dandruff is suspended in the back of his mullet, and a few King-sized Peanut M&M packs slide around the dirty pleather of the front seat. Nikki pulls out her slow smile, even touches her violet nail to her wet lip— as if about to bite it—for added effect.

The guy grunts, and the car squeals. Connecticut woods fly by. When they're let out at the station, the train's there, dirty from travel. They pay the cab driver, almost tossing the money over the seat, and jump out, grabbing their duffels. Delia's cleats clack on the asphalt as she runs across the lot. It's only when Nikki looks back that she sees the driver has a stub for his left hand, which he must have buried in his lap the whole ride. It's a pale shape. It holds the wheel now as he uses his one hand to count the money on the dash. She doesn't point it out to Delia. They hop on board, as the doors beep closed.

Delia has trouble squatting over the filthy toilet as the train rocks and jiggles. There's no more toilet paper so she uses a paper towel. She takes off her uniform, which is stuck with sweat to her skin. Pulls on her jeans, splashes her face with water, rakes her fingers through her tangled, blond hair.

As she walks down the aisle, she notices how hard Nikki's chewing her gum, looking at the moving world, the junkyards and bus lots and backyards. Nikki's face is reflected in the scratched and stained window, and she looks like a movie star, she's so beautiful.

"Yo," Delia says, thumping down onto the seat across from Nikki. "I cannot believe we made it. That was crazy."

"I knew we'd make it," she says with a blazing smile. "We had to make it."

They chitchat for a half hour, and then settle in with magazines. Delia thinks about Greg, his hand holding her hand—perfect, powerful, stunning—and how his hand would look holding Patricia's hand. She thinks of the weekend pass, and how it was a letter to Greg, in some backward way, that said: *Don't treat me right and I'll leave.* She wonders if he's found out yet that she slipped away. She wants his ears to burn with regret.

Nikki's mind flips through pictures of Seth and girls she doesn't know, specters that slip in and out of his room, girls who may or may not exist, who may or may not be sitting in his room when Nikki arrives. She even orchestrates video-gamelike battles where she and Blondie karate-chop each other in a dorm hall.

"The problem with Seth," Nikki says out of the blue, "is that he never mentions other girls. Even friends. Doesn't that seem suspicious?"

"Well, Greg just keeps talking about other girls, beyond how much he should talk about them, as if to prove there's no reason not to talk about them."

"Does he do that? I never heard him do that, I guess."

"Oh yeah. This girl Erica, who he grew up with?"

"So he told you about her?"

Delia blinks at Nikki. "What do you mean?"

Shoot. Error. "What do you mean, what do I mean?"

"How do you know her?"

"I don't know her. I met her in Fort Greene over Thanksgiving."

"So you do know her."

"No, I *met* her."

The train violently enters the pitch-black tunnel to Grand Central. They're underground.

"Why didn't you tell me about her?"

Nikki casually stands to grab her bag off the overhead rack. "I think I did," she says glibly, knowing she didn't.

Delia gets her bag too, weighing the situation. "Well, I guess I forgot."

Nikki breathes a long, silent sigh of relief.

"Oh shit, here we go," Nikki hisses as they stand in line to get off the train.

"So, we're just going to head over, yeah?"

"Yeah. I mean, if he's not there, we can wait at his

building, I guess. Or I'll call him and tell him we're here, just surprise him like that."

"Right," Delia says.

"What?" Nikki asks, thinking she picked up uncertainty.

"Nothing," Delia says. "I mean, yeah, that's what we'll do."

Outside, Manhattan hits them in the face with all its intensity, immediacy, anger, desire. It's like taking a shot of gasoline. Storefront windows glow with fur coats and black suits and leopard bags and red modern sofas and stacks of glistening china and cameras and cigars. On the soiled sidewalk, a teenager with red dreads and sores on his face slumps with his cat on a leash, a creased cardboard sign asking for bus fare back to Portland, but the guy is silent. The air has a city smell to it that's overpowering and indefinable, made of cinders and exhaust and human sweat and cologne and cigarette smoke. And there's the slight sweet tint to it from the salt water surrounding the island, and a food smell coming from the pretzel cart.

"Take a cab?" Nikki says.

Delia shrugs, and they get in the cab line.

Nikki thinks Delia looks a little lost, having only been to the city once, to see a show at Radio City Music Hall and stay at the W. She'd been shuttled from this nice venue to that, this grand room to that, and back to the airport. She hadn't seen the city. Nikki's no expert either, but she decides to act like one now.

They take the cab to 25th and First, to the Hunter dorm. They enter the large, wood-paneled lobby, where an old security guard picks his teeth behind a metal desk. Radios and CBs blink and whine on the desktop.

"Student ID," the gray-haired guy says, without looking at them.

"Um. We're here to see Seth," Delia says.

The guard rolls rheumy eyes up to meet theirs. "Seth who."

"Seth Walters," Nikki says.

The guard picks up a white intercom phone, and dials. "There's two girls here," he finally says. Then he looks at Delia and Nikki. "What's yer names?"

Delia and Nikki smile maniacally at each other, stifling laughter. Delia elbows Nikki, who then whispers: "Can you tell him just to come down to meet us?"

The guard isn't curious about or amused by the situation. "They wantcha to come down. Yeah. Yeah." He hangs up, looks at his toothpick. "He's comin'."

Nikki's confidence and aggression crested a few blocks away from here, and she's been downsliding into the feeling she had at the airport this summer, when she realized that she didn't know for sure if he really wanted to see her, or if he had stopped caring. In fact, she's fallen so far she now feels sure he'll be angry instead of overjoyed when those elevator doors open. Her butterflies have closed their wings, and sit in her bowels like stones. Apricot-lit numbers count down the floors as the car descends, and Nikki tries desperately to compose her face.

A *bing* and the door clatters open. There he is: hat turned backward, long-sleeved Oakley shirt, nylon athletic pants, flip-flops. His eyes scan the lobby and don't even pick up the girls, as they're impossible visitors. When he locks eyes with Nikki, a smile of amazement creeps onto his strong face.

"Holy *shit*," he says.

"Surprise," Nikki says in a deadpan voice, but she's smiling too.

"Holy, holy *shit*," he says again, now starting to walk toward them. "And you brought your partner in crime," he says, shaking his head.

When he hugs Nikki, she inhales deeply.

"Georgie, these girls can come in whenever they like," Seth tells the guard.

"Yeah yeah, if they sign in, that is, smart guy."

"These are the best girls that ever signed in," Seth tells the old man.

"Yeah, well, tell them to stay that way," the guard says, lifting one end of his mouth in what seems to be a gesture of a smile.

Seth ushers the girls into the elevator, and tells them

Georgie is a hard-ass but softens over time. The car rises, and all three look at one another. Seth shakes his head again.

"How on *earth* did you two rig this up?"

Nikki and Delia look at each other with conspirators' grins. They shrug.

"It's a secret," Delia says. "We have our ways."

Nikki notices that Seth is nervous. Almost smaller, almost dwarfed by the gigantic building, the indifferent security guard, the buzz and clang of lives being lived all around—extreme lives, lives past any threshold these three have imagined, lives they couldn't dream up if their own lives depended on it.

Nikki squeezes Seth's hand.

He looks at her crookedly, unsurely, still in shock. "Where are you guys staying?" he asks.

Nikki tries to laugh. "With you, dumb-ass."

He opens his eyes wide. "Are you serious?"

Delia reins in the awkward moment. "Two ladies in your room, Seth. Can you handle it?"

The door chimes, and they step out. Seth points them to the right, and they walk down the dirty-carpeted hall. Smells of popcorn, musty towels, smoke, and beer stains hang like mist. Seth opens Room 67, warning them that the place isn't exactly clean.

The girls are, in fact, taken aback. The tiny cell is crowded with aluminum take-out containers, used textbooks, ashtrays, malt liquor bottles, dirty clothes. A basket-ball. No chairs. A laptop on a small desk. A bed.

"Whoa," Nikki says.

But secretly she's pleased. No self-respecting girls are spending time in this pit. And it means this really was one of the reasons he didn't want Nikki to visit. He hadn't been lying. When Delia goes to the loo, Nikki grabs her chance.

"I guess now's as good a time as any to ask you about the blond girl over Thanksgiving," she says, and her eyes get hard.

Seth looks at her in surprise. "With shoulder-length hair, and bangs? Skinny?"

Nikki nods. "I saw pictures of her wearing your wind-breaker at the bonfire party."

Seth smiles. "I'm so busted. That's my cousin, you idiot."

Nikki's frozen. Then she starts to laugh, and can hardly stop. When Delia gets back, Seth shrugs at her, points to the giggling mess. "I told her about my cousin, who's a blonde."

Delia's smile breaks slowly. "At the bonfire, right? Is that who that was?"

Nikki's laughing too hard to answer, but she nods. She's laughing in a kind of manic embarrassment.

They decide on a twelve-pack of Budweiser and potato chips. Seth goes down to buy the beer with his new fake ID while the girls hang out. Delia showers in the coed bathroom, which feels bizarre.

Nikki straightens up a bit, but doesn't want to seem like she was snooping. When he comes back, both girls are lounging on his bed, listening to his iPod attached to speakers, singing along to the Scissor Sisters.

"Hope you're thirsty, we got to drink these before they get warm," he says, smiling slyly. "I don't have a fridge yet."

Delia cracks one open and rolls her eyes as if the smell makes her deliriously happy. "God bless you, Seth."

They toast, clacking the cans together, and drink foam out of the keyhole. And slowly, eventually, they relax.

They end up at a Mexican restaurant that doesn't card. They get a pitcher of frozen guava margarita, and the frothy, icy stuff is lethal. Like a kid's drink. The guacamole is homemade too, and the three of them glaze over with pleasure. Seth's phone rings, and he gives someone the address of where they are.

"Who was that?" Nikki asks.

"My friend Teddy. You guys will like him, he's insane."

"He's at Hunter?" Delia asks.

"Yeah, from fucking Ohio originally. And from the stories I've heard, his town was just too small for him. So he got moved to an aunt's house in New Jersey for his two last years of high school."

When Teddy shows up, he struts in with a smirk. He's

got an eighties-British-rock-star thing going. A devious, beautiful face like David Bowie. Clothes that look permanent, as if he sleeps in them. Tweed blazer with shredded lapels, glossed-back hair. A gold skull ring on his finger.

"These are the stowaways, are they?" he asks.

Delia is too shy to answer.

"I guess we are," Nikki says brightly, already fighting not to slur—the candy drinks have caught up.

Teddy sits down, grinning ear to ear. "Well, we should make it a special night, then."

They order fajitas and another pitcher, and they toast one another again. The restaurant is dark, small, and they're in a back niche. Red chili pepper lights are strung along the dark walls, and candles flicker on their table. When the fajitas come, the plates sizzle and steam, and everyone digs in, making a commotion.

"Let's go rock and roll," Teddy says after another pitcher, when their greasy napkins are crumpled on their place mats.

Delia is tipsy enough to look at him directly. He's slightly ridiculous, but also magnetic. And he's demonstrating such enthusiasm for the girls being here, and showing them a good time, and shoring up his boy Seth—it's hard not to like him.

They stand outside the Continental, where Teddy swears they can get in because he knows the bouncer. But when they get up in the line, it's a different guy.

"Where's Ray?" he asks.

The guy shrugs, shines his flashlight on the IDs of the next people in line.

"I'm here all the time," Teddy says. "I'm just bringing my buddies in to check out these bands."

"Sure," the bouncer says, shifting his substantial haunches on his wooden stool. "With proper ID and cover charge, they're all in."

Teddy looks hopelessly at the girls, who almost imperceptibly shake their heads.

Seth buys a pint of Jack Daniel's at a liquor store, and they walk through the streets, laughing, pushing one another, swigging from the bottle in the brown paper bag. Whenever Teddy tells a story, he makes them stop so he can do impressions. Nikki feels amazing, better than she's felt in her whole life, walking these wild streets, walking next to her boyfriend past windows of bars that quake with bass, past iron-gated parks where owners are still out, throwing balls for their pit bulls, past enormous building after building.

She keeps thinking: *No one knows where I am. I'm unrecorded. Free.*

They end up in Teddy's room in the dorm, one flight above Seth's. His room is neat as a pin, with vintage posters of obscure punk bands on the walls. He lights incense, and they sit around while he goes through his computer for music to play. Everyone shouts to be heard, and Delia kicks over the Jack Daniel's, and Teddy forgives her, sops it out of the carpet with paper towels. Seth burps Mexican, and Nikki yells at him.

"You guys want to try this stuff?" Teddy asks suddenly, pawing through his desk drawer.

"What is it?" Nikki says.

"Oh shit, I smoked this," Seth says. "Be careful."

Teddy packs his glass bong, delicately pressing blue-haired bud into the bowl. Delia and Nikki look at each other. Teddy tells them he'll pull some smoke, and they can take a tiny hit each. He lights the bud, and it glows a pure and crackling orange. When Nikki sips from the glass tube, she inhales too much and coughs.

"Uh-oh," Seth says, smiling. He has the greasy-eyed look he gets when he's drunk.

Nikki smiles with lopsided chagrin and waits to see how bad it will be. Almost immediately, the room starts to shift. Delia smokes, and Nikki smiles at her, wanting to say something but finding her mouth glued shut. Teddy is manically looking at his computer for the next song, the screen's blue light making his eyes burn coldly.

Nikki hangs in there, seeing the three of them as though they're far away.

Seth looks at her. "Sleepy, kid?" he says finally, quiet enough for the other two not to hear.

She nods. He helps her up. Delia stops talking and looks at Nikki. They both know what crossroads this is. Nikki wants Seth's room to be theirs alone; she only has one night. She feels guilty and weird for being ruthless, but she'd do anything to get Delia to stay here.

"Um," Delia starts, still looking deep at Nikki.

"What do you want to do, babe?" Nikki says, knowing she just threw a loaded question right between Delia's eyes. "Do you want to come by later?" Nikki also knows the weak tone she used for the second part of the question communicated how badly she wants Delia never to come by.

Delia nods, at first slowly, then with better sincerity. "Sure. I'll be down in a while." Then she turns to Teddy. "If that's cool with you."

Teddy puts on a blandly innocent face. "Of course."

Nikki and Seth take the stairs down one floor. On the wall are painted institutional floor numbers. When they get to his room, weaving, Nikki strips to her shirt and underwear, and jumps in bed to get warm.

He climbs in, presses against her. He reaches back to click off the light. They kiss slowly, luxuriously, as the city beeps and barks and rings outside.

"I can't believe you're here," he whispers into her neck.

She smiles woozily, kisses what she thinks will be his mouth but is his nose. He laughs, but something about the darkness and the fact that he's on top of her is combining badly. The room is spinning. A big dark twirl. She pushes him off.

"Hold on," she says.

She gets up. She runs to the bathroom in her shirt and underwear, barefoot, and spends some quality time on her knees in front of the john. Seth comes in but doesn't knock on her stall.

"Hey, babe, you okay?"

"Yeah, yeah," she lies. "Just making sure. Thought I might be sick."

He hesitates because he must know she's lying, but leaves her. After she's done, she steps out and wets a paper towel with cold water to cool down her boiling face. She looks at herself in the mirror, half dressed, makeup blurred. Suddenly the door swings open.

A goth guy walks in, his black leather overcoat nearly dragging on the white tile floor. Safety pins in his eyebrow. One eye made yellow with a contact lens. He's got a toothbrush and a tube of Colgate in his hands, and his nails are painted black.

"Um," Nikki says. "Can I get a swipe of your toothpaste?"

He looks her up and down. "Sure," he says, friendly as any good neighbor, and holds out the tube.

Pigeons murmur and shuffle on the ledge outside, and the morning seeps into the room like dust from their wings.

Nikki spoons the back of Seth, who was asleep by the time she returned to his room last night. She kisses his spine and he makes a noise: It's a sign of acknowledgment but also a no-thank-you.

She keeps trying until he groans. "Dude, my head," he whispers, and she realizes his hangover must be too bad to even talk aloud.

She pulls on her jeans, gets him Gatorade from the hall vending machine, and finds Advil Liqui-Gels in his drawer. "Here, baby."

"Oh my God, thank you," he says into the mattress, reaching his hand blindly for the medicine.

"I'm going to get Delia."

"Go get Delia," he agrees. "We'll have brunch or something when I can see straight."

Nikki takes the stairs, the steps freezing on her bare feet. She's cloaked in shame. The dirty carpet says it all.

She knocks on Teddy's door. There's nothing. She wonders if they went for breakfast. She feels shitty about the night, making her stay down here. "Hey, you guys," she calls into the seam of the door.

Now she hears a grunt and a rustle. She thinks they've said come in, which is why she opens the door. But Delia shouts crudely at her to get out.

"I said 'wait a minute,' for fuck's sake!"

And Nikki wishes she had. Then she wouldn't have seen

Delia's breasts as she tried to get enough blanket to cover herself, or Teddy's bare back, or the orange Trojan wrapper next to the mattress. She wouldn't have met Delia's eye the way she did, without censoring herself, she wouldn't have looked at her friend with raw disgust.

20

The train creeps along rusty tracks, taking its sweet time up the Harlem Line. Normally, a slow train is what every student hopes for when returning. Most students onboard are praying for a blizzard or train malfunction, anything to postpone the Sunday-night reality monster. Not Nikki. A bullet train couldn't get her back fast enough. This morning's mixture of greasy eggs and coffee only amplified the hangover. And yet she also doesn't want to get back to school. Not today. Not ever.

Nikki glares at Delia, sprawled on the opposite seat. *How can she sleep like nothing happened?* They haven't talked about last night. They made chitchat—through blaring migraines—with Seth and Teddy at the diner. Tried to be cute and tried to keep their toast and jam down. Not like the boys were doing better. Seth's eye sockets were deep and green, and Teddy kept belching and then excusing himself. It was lovely.

Delia may look asleep to Nikki, but she hasn't had any rest. The seat next to her appears empty, but Mr. Scary Demon is sitting there, whispering in Delia's ear possible excuses and explanations for what happened, and then laughing as if even *he* can't buy them. Greg is certain not to believe her.

Nikki watches the conductor make another pass in their car, checking tickets wedged in the seats.

"Paw-*ling*," he calls out in that old-fashioned fish-peddling voice.

Delia opens her eyes slowly. She stretches like a cat and yawns widely without covering her mouth. Delia looks dissolutely at Nikki.

"Nik, I don't want to go back there."

Nikki smiles crookedly, sadly. "Me neither."

Delia looks out at the cold, brown fields. Uneven wire fencing keeps goats close to a rickety house.

"Let's get off at the next stop."

"But we've got four more stops to Glendon."

Delia tugs at her hair and looks at the ceiling in frustration, but then she speaks softly. "I know, Nik. I know. But God, we don't technically have to be back until Check In tonight. We have this, like, bit of freedom left, right? I don't know. I think we should take it."

The train is applying its brakes in anticipation of the stop.

Nik's blood pressure is rising. "What will we do?"

The train stops, the doors open. *Beep. Beep.*

Delia smiles for the first time since they left the guys. "Whatever we want."

Nikki smiles back. They madly scramble their stuff together, leaving soda cans and magazines on the seat, slipping through the doors just before they close.

The girls walk down the stairs off the cement platform as the train shrilly calls its way through the next intersection. They're almost skipping. There's hope they'll each make up for what was, in the end, a disappointing, difficult weekend.

Pawling is infamous for its State Psychiatric Hospital perched on the hill above town, a gothic compound with razor wire surrounding the buildings and bars in the windows. The hospital has been closed for over a decade, but it still haunts the village. The girls look at it now, and the entrapment and eeriness of the hospital's shell fuels their lightheadedness at being free.

Neither has ever been here, and there's a reason. The town practically doesn't exist anymore. The one stoplight blinks a steady orange on the one main street, which seems deserted. The only life are rumors of flickering hospital lights residents swear they see, a cluster of dirty, shoebox-sized houses at the street's end, and a few shops here at the main crossroads—including the primary drinking hole marked with a red neon BAR sign.

They look at each other.

"I don't have ID," Nikki says.

"I don't think it matters."

The bar is windowless and smoky, with a jukebox by the door and a dartboard in the back. No heads turn when Delia opens the door. Two men hunch over drinks, fixed on the Giants game on the small TV. A lady with white-lavender hair is staring at her glass; under her trench coat is a calico housedress. The way she moves her lips over her gums means she has no teeth.

The girls walk to the bar. Delia orders two Budweisers and two shots of Southern Comfort from a grizzly bartender. She holds up a twenty. Nikki holds her breath.

The bartender glances at the girls and pulls two beers from the icy cooler, reaches for the Southern Comfort and pours shots into slightly unclean glasses. Delia slides the twenty and the bartender hands over the drinks.

"No change." Delia smiles.

The girls find a round table in the corner. "Oh, shit," Nikki hisses in weird exhilaration. "That was stupidly easy."

Delia smiles and raises her shot to toast. "To best friends," she says.

Nikki clinks. "To best friends."

And that's it. They both agree without saying anything about it, that they'll just continue on this roller coaster, not discuss the elephant in the room. Not this afternoon. Maybe not ever. It means that at the core of their friendship something is rotten, and it means that neither one will completely trust the other, but they can stay friends without having a terrible conversation. Without risking everything. They can do it the safe way.

Nikki buys the second round.

Delia lifts her shot glass. "Here's to stealing the afternoon."

They toss it back and chase it with Budweiser. Nikki wipes her mouth. Delia shakes her head. They laugh.

Nikki gets change for a few dollars and hits the jukebox, plays *Exile on Main St.* in its entirety. At the table, the girls sing together along with "Sweet Virginia." *"Come on, come on down, Sweet Virginia . . . uh-huh. You got to scrape the shit right off your shoe."*

An older guy in a plaid shirt and jeans sidles up with his thumbs in his belt loops like a cartoon. He challenges the girls to a game of darts. Before Nikki can say no, Delia hops out of her seat.

"Let's do it, I'll kick your ass," Delia shouts, and her mouth is wet in the way it gets when she's getting drunk.

Nikki protests, but Delia is dancing her way toward the

dartboard, singing along still: *"Come on, come on down, you got it in you,"* Delia playfully motions for Nikki to join her. *"Got to scrape that shit right off your shoes."*

Dale's thirty-two, or so he says, and he was a registered nurse at the psych hospital. Now he's a home care worker. Delia winks at Nikki and tells Dale he sure looks like the toughest nurse she's ever seen. Dale laughs without looking at them. They play Cricket, and Delia wins each time. Her brothers taught her a thing or two about darts.

Buying another round, Nikki and Delia look at each other blearily, slyly. They're in a weird zone, where nothing matters, where they run it all. This bar. This town. This night. They're kings of this moment. Wellington barely exists; they've outrun it.

Although the clock on the wall says it's six thirty. They both realize the other is looking at it.

"Hey, sir?" Nikki says to the bartender. "When's the next train leave?"

"From where to where?" he asks smugly.

"You know, like, from here to go up. To go north."

The trench coat lady answers the question without looking up from stirring her drink. "You missed 'em all."

Delia and Nikki almost giggle, look covertly at each other.

"Um, *no*, we know there's a couple more tonight," Delia informs the lady as politely as she can.

The lady's mouth, when she turns to speak to them, is a sunken cave. "Ya read the weekday schedule," she says. "It's Sunday."

"No more trains north," the bartender confirms as he dries glasses with a damp rag.

Delia and Nikki end up in the ladies' room, tilting and giggling as they try to pee. In the corner of one stall is a tampon, brown with dried blood. They put on lipstick in the mirror, pushing each other playfully out of the way.

"Dude," Nikki says, pressing her sticky lips together. "What the hell we gone do?"

Delia laughs and points at her. "Shit, dude, you're slurring."

"What are we going to *do*?" Nikki asks, adamant as a little girl who wants someone to take care of things.

Delia shrugs, the devil glowing in her eye. "Let's call Somerset. Tell him we got stuck in town. Bomb scare in Grand Central, I don't know."

Nikki's eyes gleam, and the girls stare at each other in the mirror. "He could find that out on the news, though."

"No, stuff like that happens in airports and whatever all the time these days. Or we could tell him my dad needs to see me for one more night, because we had a bad fight. It's really important." Here she makes a sad face. "I'm the child of divorce, Nik. It's hard."

"Oh, shit," Nikki says, smiling and looking away, knowing they're going to stay. Loving it. They both set fire to this thing. They both enjoy watching it burn.

They get Dale to call from Nikki's phone and leave a message on Somerset's voice mail. They coach him in the foyer to the bathrooms, away from the music. All huddled, high on fear and courage, in this stinking hall.

"Sound like my father," Delia keeps telling him.

"Well, I don't know how your father *sounds*," he keeps reminding her.

"Well," Nikki suggests. "Sound like *a* father."

The night is not the same after. They keep drinking until the room is unsteady as a ship's deck. A man honks an ancient mint-green Chevy outside, and the trench coat lady groans and grumbles, making her way to its open passenger-side door. Dale is overly impressed with his own performance and keeps repeating parts of his Somerset speech. And the girls seem, to anyone looking, to be having as much fun as they were before. They're still the flamboyant center of attention. But before they'd been pushing the envelope; things feel different now that they've taken that envelope and ripped it into pieces.

The unthinkable happens around ten. Nikki orders two more beers and is having trouble getting the bills out of her wallet. She drops coins that go pinging and twirling on the floor.

"You two are done," the bartender says, casually turning

the pages of his horse-racing paper.

Nikki freezes. "Ex-s-scuse me?"

"You've had your last drink here," he says non-confrontationally.

Nikki does a formal pirouette back to Delia, whispers in her ear.

Delia glares at the bartender, and says loud enough for him to hear that she can't believe she was tipping him all night. He doesn't flinch at all.

The girls strategize in their irrational way, interrupting each other. Nikki suggests they take a cab all the way back, and Delia reminds her they're supposed to still be in New York. Delia asks where there's a good place to stay, and Dale laughs. There's only one place in town, the Motel 6, up the road. After more haggling with each other and counting of money, the girls start packing up. Dale offers to drive them but Nikki promptly refuses, saying fresh air would do them good.

"See ya later, Dale the dart-man!" Delia shouts on their way out of the bar.

They strut past the bartender in dignified rejection, and then Nikki trips as she crosses the threshold. As the door shuts, Nikki hears Dale say something but doesn't care what it was.

The empty street is dully sparkling, glazed with cold. The girls weave and laugh, further burdened with their luggage on their shoulders. The Main Street stores are dismal, half of them boarded up or simply empty, except for a wig head turned over in the storefront, or a handwritten sign taped to the door: FOR RENT: CALL BOBBY AT SUNSET. They pass a liquor store, an OTB, a stationery shop with goods in the window so faded they look like they've been soaking up sun there for decades. The hospital lights, those ever-present beacons in this town, twinkle like stars.

"Man," Delia says. "If I ever go crazy, I'll be *real* pissed they put me there."

Nikki laughs. "You already are crazy, Deals."

"Play *nice*, Nicole," Delia says like a schoolteacher. "We're in this together."

The fluorescent-lighted lobby of the motel is rank with an unspecified odor. They parade through with invincible pluck. They lean up on the front desk and give their adult smiles.

The man behind the desk scratches the eczema on his elbow as he welcomes them. "We're glad you chose Motel Six tonight, my name is Lance." His radio is tuned to a gospel station. He assigns them Room 18, on the first floor, and hands them a key. Delia haggles with him about offering free HBO but not Showtime, just to demonstrate bravado. The bravado is draining.

"Don't you like *Weeds*?" Delia laughs, but her joke is lost on Lance.

When they reach their room, Nikki collapses on the floral

comforter of the lone queen bed.

"I wouldn't go near that comforter if I were you." Delia lays her bag on the desk and moves to the window, which looks on to the parking lot, to drop the blinds.

"I'm too exhausted to care," Nikki answers.

But she does drag herself up to brush her teeth. The drinking, especially on top of the hangover, has settled into her like a poison. It's visible in her gray face, and her eye makeup is blurred, her mouth pale. She uses the glass, overturned on the scalloped paper coaster, to try some water, but her body doesn't want it.

"I am so *shredded*," she complains as she falls into the bed.

Delia is already under the covers watching TV, eyes half-closed. Nikki wonders if Delia is pretending sleep so that there's no chance of talking about last night, or Boston, or rumors—now that they're in a small room by themselves. If she is, that's fine, because Nikki doesn't want to talk either.

But Delia's not faking. She's succumbing to many hours of alcohol, which feel like dirty cotton batting around her skull. They're watching MTV with the sound off, and the silent rock stars seem fallible and small, jumping and making belligerent faces and threatening gestures. The girls fall asleep with the lights on.

A knock startles them awake, and neither knows the time, how long they've been out. The world through the thin slits of their blinds is still black. The room is bright.

"Hello?" Delia says quietly, her voice unsteady.

"Hey." A deep, friendly voice comes through the thin pine door. "It's Dale."

"Who?" Delia asks.

"Dale," he says with a slow smile in his voice. "Dale the Dart-Man."

"Oh." Delia looks confused about what to do. Nikki grabs Delia's arm, preventing her from getting out of bed.

"Dale, we're already sleeping," Nikki tries. "We're tired."

"You sure? You guys don't want to hang out?"

"Yeah, we're sure," Nikki says in what she hopes is a jovial voice.

"Goodnight, Dale," Delia calls out.

"Aw, shoot," Dale says with what sounds like genial disappointment. "All right, then. Goodnight, ladies."

After a minute of barely breathing, they still don't hear him, and so Nikki jumps up, tiptoes to the door to check all the locks, and then hurries back. The girls sit quietly in the bed for a minute until Nikki breaks the silence. "What a freakin' weirdo." She tries laughing.

But Delia's face doesn't change. "How did he know what room we're in?"

Nikki's heartbeat picks up speed. "Let's call the front desk."

Lance picks up. He says he knows Dale and not to worry, the guy is harmless. "Everyone knows each other in this town," Lance assures them.

"But how did he know where we were?" Delia asks unsurely, biting her cuticle.

"Well, Holy Mary, come to think of it, I guess I don't know," Lance says brightly.

The girls lie in fetal positions facing each other, the covers pulled up to their chins.

"Do you think Lance told him?" Delia whispers.

"I don't know."

"Why would he, right?"

"I can't imagine. Are we being paranoid?"

"Do you think he followed us?" Delia says after a moment.

"He could have."

Delia thinks again. "Should we call the police?"

Nikki shudders. "Dude, do you know how much trouble we'll be in? We'll be expelled."

"You think?"

"No, I *know*. For a fact."

Another knock. This time neither girl moves a muscle.

"Come on, gals, why don't you all let me in?" Dale's voice amiably pleads. "I was just thinking, why don't we party a little more?"

The girls breathe.

"I mean," he says smoothly, "here I helped you out and all, and you won't even talk to me."

Nikki can't hold back. "Listen, we're calling the police right now!"

Delia looks at her friend, asking with her eyes. Nikki shakes her head.

Dale is silent. Then he chuckles like an old man about to tell his favorite story. "Well, now, don't do that."

After a moment, they hear his heavy boots trudge down the hall.

Delia slides out of bed, turning off lights and looking furtively through the blinds. All she sees is a blue pickup and a beat-up white Nissan in the lot. Delia can't remember if both were there before. She climbs underneath the covers. "Was there a white car in the parking lot when we checked in, Nik?"

"I'm not sure. I wasn't really paying attention." Nikki is curled up facing away from Delia. She feels ill.

"Fuck, dude," Delia says, staring at the ceiling.

Maybe five minutes later, it happens. Two beams of lights—headlights—are being pointed into their room, and because the blinds don't close completely, shards of light slice up the bed. The girls shield their faces, trying to see the moving vehicle. It's getting closer, until it parks not more than ten feet away. The engine's cut. The lights stay on.

Now Delia feels her limbs quake. She swallows.

Nikki slips out of the bed, like a soldier, squat-walking to stay under the window sill. There are curtains, too, and

245

she tries to drag them closed, but they're jammed. She kneels on the floor, her eyes big and wet in the strange light. She beckons for Delia to get off the bed.

"He can see you," she mouths.

Delia drops onto the floor and makes her way to Nikki. They look at each other for an answer, both of them shivering. Their faces look old.

They kneel there, their knees getting hard, holding hands, and wait for the lights to leave. The lights stay on. Nikki slumps down, sits cross-legged, puts her hand over her face. Delia has an idea and drags the comforter and sheet off the bed, collects them in the unlit corner of the room.

"What are you doing?" Nikki whispers.

"We can try to sleep where he can't see us."

They lie on the floor, Nikki spooning Delia for warmth, the sheets and blankets a mess around them. Delia's crying, and Nikki reaches around to rub the hot tears off her friend's cheek.

"I want it to be morning," Delia says in a thick voice.

"I know, baby," Nikki says.

The lights last all night, and neither girl sleeps. When dawn comes, it washes away those two beams with its own light, and at some point the vehicle slips back into the town, into the new day.

21

The train car is overheated. Delia's face is flushed, and she's pressing her forehead to the cool window. God, they've been gone for two nights, but it feels like a month. The girls couldn't find a coffee shop or anything before they got on the train so their stomachs are making ominous noises. All they ate last night was beer and liquor. Delia looks at her dirty fingernails.

They've said little to each other. Delia sneaks looks at Nikki, who's splayed on the seat, almost snoring. And now they're pulling up to the Glendon platform, so Delia shakes her. Her friend wakes up and gives an immediately scornful look. Delia grits her teeth. *Why do I feel like the bad one?*

As the train heaves its metal components to a screeching

stop, Nikki looks blearily out the doors. There's Somerset, breathing plumes of cold, his tie blown behind his shoulder. He's looking into the doors, his eyes flicking, searching for his advisees. Delia turns to Nikki, and they both have the same desperate expression.

"Hey, there," Delia calls out as she steps into the morning. She tries to project casual regret, nothing profound. No exhaustion. No fear.

Somerset's jaw clenches and unclenches.

Nikki waves weakly. "We didn't know you'd be picking us up."

The wind howls through the threesome as they meet. There are no cars in the Glendon parking lot except for Somerset's, and it almost shivers in the strong wind.

"I met the other two trains this morning, not sure which one you'd come in on," he says in a flat voice. "Since you don't have your phones on."

They follow him, looking at each other behind his broad back. He opens the back of the car, and they carefully stow their luggage.

"Well, it's really nice of you," Delia says timidly.

He turns to them. "I'm not being nice. You could have gotten me fired with this, this, whatever it is."

"We didn't—" Nikki begins to explain.

He puts a hand up immediately. "Tell me this. Are you both okay?"

They nod, hoping he's turning back into the Somerset they know.

"Did either of you do anything that could endanger yourself in the future?"

"I don't know what that means," Delia says, shrugs shyly, hoping to come off a bit funny.

"Goddamnit, you do know what it means. Unsafe sex. Needles, violence—"

"Jesus, Somerset, what are you talking about?" Nikki laughs, angry or embarrassed.

"I'm responsible for whatever happened this weekend. I need to know if I need to worry. Do you understand?" he spits out.

Nikki and Delia look at each other.

Somerset interrupts them before they begin. "I don't want to know what you did or where you were. I need to know if you're okay or not. And then we will not discuss this again. You were with your father in New York. You stayed an extra night with my permission because the circumstances were extreme." He looks at each of them. "And it's *Mister* Somerset."

The girls both sit in the backseat, like they're eight. The ride back to school is about fifteen minutes, plus a hundred years long. The frozen pastures bristle, like nappy hide. The houses look at the girls with dark, square eyes. Nikki thinks of Seth, and the fact that each minute they drive, they drive farther away from him.

For some reason, Nikki also thinks of Hannah, Somerset's almost-girlfriend, and how she took down her red braids. But she didn't love him. And she thinks of the disfigured arm of the cabdriver, and how she had told him to drive faster. She thinks of Gabriel, his Creed cologne, the Italian watch, the tassels on his loafers. She remembers the first time he formally pulled her chair out for her in the dining hall, and she made fun of him in front of everyone, and he never did it again.

The girls drop their bags in their rooms, and as instructed, go straight to class. Leaving the dorm, they shake their heads, too tired and distraught to speak. Each girl blames the other.

Of course, Nikki's first class is poli sci. She rakes her hands through her hair as she takes her seat. She feels like the sins of the weekend are written all over her in black marker. Gabriel walks in as the bell rings, and he looks at her across the big round table. His chin tilted up in resigned curiosity.

After class, she moves toward him. He stands apart from her.

"Why didn't you tell me you were heading out for the weekend?" he says simply.

"It was short notice," she mumbles, knowing he

deserves a better explanation.

He looks at her, books held against his side with one big hand, waiting. His leather belt is secured with a monogrammed silver buckle. His jacket sits on his big square shoulders. Suddenly, Nikki feels heat behind her eyes. Water in her mouth. She's going to cry. Gabriel puts his arm over her shoulders, directs her through the halls.

They find an empty classroom in the math wing. Nikki sits down. An abacus sits on the teacher's desk, its beads glinting in the sun. Chalk dust hangs in the air.

"You went to go see Seth," Gabriel says, sitting at a desk next to her.

And then Nikki cries. Her tears are dirty, and all she wants is to take a scorching shower and crawl into her bed. When she's done crying, she hiccups.

Gabriel is looking out the window. "You always pull away from me. Like, when I touch you."

Nikki cringes. His gentle way is worse than getting yelled at. She hiccups again. "*Gabriel.* You're the only gentleman in this class."

He looks at her blankly.

"You're a better person than me," she blubbers on.

"What does that have to do with anything?" he asks.

Nikki looks at the floor, so beat up she's almost high. "I don't know," she admits.

Because the problem is *she always pulls away from him.*

And she decides to explain Seth. Lay all the cards on the table, and let Gabriel choose his hand.

He looks out the window as she talks (and hiccups). Nikki tells him about this summer, the bonfire, the pool room. She tells him now about the dorm, the paranoia, how drunk she got, puking in the stall. He winces at some of it and looks blankly through the rest.

The bell rings. A class starts meandering into the room. One girl looks inquisitively at the couple.

Gabriel stretches as he stands. "It's okay," he tells the girl. "We're done."

A freak ice storm hits Glendon. Both girls are overjoyed; it means Woods Crew is canceled, and soccer practice is just an hour of watching plays on the coaching room TV. Delia knows Greg is looking for her, a few people tell her so. But she can't talk to him—her mind is toxic and beaten. Both girls take burning showers and fall asleep before dinner, sleep to the next morning.

Delia dreams of Greg. The dream is long, tortured, complicated. There's a jukebox, but she can't find a quarter, and he's mad. Then she puts on a song, and he asks her, suspicious, how she knows this punk rock band. She knows that he knows everything. There's a lot more to the dream, but the only other part she remembers on waking is staring at a car, whose headlights are directed at her. She's cupping her hand over her eyes, trying to see who's driving. The car is slowly moving toward her but she wants to see, so she doesn't move. And there, now, she makes out the face: It's Greg.

When Delia wakes up, she still feels like she got hit by a truck, but it's not the same as yesterday. She's putting her jacket on when she looks out the window and sees the glass world. When she'd gone to bed last night, the world was ordinary. Now it's encased in ice. The Japanese maple out the window clacks in the wind, its few remaining red leaves like ornaments.

As she straightens her hat in the mirror, Delia performs a little exercise. She forces herself to see that the reflection is her. If only she could know how many times this experiment has been performed in the mirrors throughout this dorm. The electricity of identity crackles through the rooms.

Of course, walking out of the dorm, she sees Greg before she sees anyone else. He and Noah are skating on the lawn in their Timberlands. He senses her presence across the green, and stops short, arms flailing, and looks her way.

She halts under the Japanese maple, terrified.

"Deals," he barks, his voice slicing the cold air.

She stands there. He comes running, Noah watching.

Greg's arms in his black jacket pumping, his face under a wool cap gleaming in the icy morning. When he gets to her, he's breathing steam like a dragon.

"Deals," he says again, panting.

She doesn't know where to begin, what to apologize for. Should she start with this past summer, the glass door, the orange juice? Or just stick to Teddy, his narrow thighs, the stale-smoke-perfumed duvet, the comic books on his floor? Perhaps she should try to communicate the more nebulous stuff, the paranoia and fantasies of vengeance and dreams of loyalty.

"I'm sorry," Greg says.

Wait a minute, this is backward, Delia thinks. "For what?"

"It was so messed up what I said."

Delia starts to melt. "I shouldn't have gone."

"What happened, are you okay? What the hell were you guys thinking?" His concern shows an edge.

"Oh, man," Delia says, looking away. "We shouldn't have gone."

"What happened?" he asks again, large arms crossed across his chest.

"Baby, I have to get to class. I seriously can't screw up this morning. Can we meet later?"

Greg nods, inventorying her with his eyes. "Um, how about the observatory, like eight thirty?"

"We'll talk," she says.

"We'll talk," he says, and he smiles and turns away, hollers to Noah.

Delia and Nikki see each other later that day on the path to Somerset's. They got green slips to come meet with him. They trudge along the icy path in which salt balls have burned pocks. Their shoes have tidemarks of the salt on them.

"What do you think?" Delia asks.

Nikki shakes her head. "I don't know. I mean, he didn't want to know before, why would he want to know now? Right?"

Delia shrugs. "Yeah. I mean, I don't know what else to think."

Somerset opens the door into his warm apartment. He's cordial. "Come in, come in," he says as he always used to do.

Hot chocolate simmers on the stove, and he adds little marshmallows, a few of which he spills in nervousness. The girls sit on the couch.

They sip the hot chocolate. Somerset smiles, but at the floor. "Girls," he says to the carpet, "I think you're both great students. I really like you as people, I will say that."

"But?" Nikki asks.

"But I shouldn't be your advisor next semester. Or next year." He ducks his head to sip from his mug, avoiding their eyes.

Delia leans forward. "But we want you to be."

Somerset licks his lips, and then looks at her. "I don't want to be."

"Oh my God," Nikki fumes as they walk back to the dorm, stunned. Her cheeks are red from cold and rage. "I get dumped by Gabriel this morning. And by my advisor this afternoon. Fucking unreal."

"It's crazy," Delia murmurs.

"What is going *on*? I mean, Jesus. What the hell?" Nikki continues.

"I don't know," Delia says.

They're in front of the dorm when Nikki hits a slick spot and does a Charlie Chaplin move, flailing her arms like windmill blades as she tries to regain balance. Delia can't help but laugh, but when Nikki gets straight, she turns on her.

"Shut *up*! You *bitch*!" Nikki grabs ice and twigs from the ground and throws them at Delia, but they don't reach her. Her face looks like a wolf. She's equal parts ugly and comical. "No wonder you got fucking banned from your own town, you ruin *everything*."

This last part stops Delia cold. She lets Nikki stomp up the stone stoop of the building. Her friend slams the door, or tries to; it has a mechanism to prevent that. Delia looks at the ground, where squirrels are raking through the shrubs for anything to eat.

And then she runs up after Nikki. She busts into Nikki's room without knocking. Nikki's just standing there in the middle of the room, wild-eyed, unsure what to do with her anger.

"I did not get banned from my town," Delia says evenly.

"You're such a *liar*!" Nikki shrieks.

"I have never once lied to you, Nik." Delia's voice shakes.

"Ha!" Nikki says, with sarcasm. "You told me those rumors weren't true."

"About the football team? The beach gangbang? Please. None of that shit was true. That's like someone's effed-up fantasy."

"I can't believe you're going to lie to me again," Nikki purrs with menace.

"I did do something that got me in trouble. It wasn't any of those things," Delia says quietly.

Nikki finally has nothing to say.

Delia sits on her bed, takes her mittens off. Holds the baby-blue knit mittens in her hands and looks at them. "I'll tell you, but you can't tell anyone." She looks up at Nikki.

Nikki sits on the other bed. Her face shows trepidation, as if she might not, after all, want to know. She rubs her gold charms between her fingertips. "I won't."

Delia pulls her hair from her face. "Oh, man. So I was at my friend Rachel's house. Her house is crazy, it's, like, built into a cliff. You look right out at the water."

Nikki nods vaguely.

"But she only lived there sometimes, with her mom and stepdad, and the rest of the time with her real dad. Her mom's a freak, used to do drugs, she produces movies and stuff. And her husband, Gerald, is crazy too. He works on movies too, but he's, like, younger than her, and he makes half the money."

Delia now looks at Nikki to see if she's already judging. "Go ahead," Nikki says.

"They have a whole gym suite. And they have a steam room. We loved it, me and Rachel, after we went early-morning surfing or whatever. Steam your body.

"Gerald came in with us sometimes. He surfed with us. And I don't know, I guess I flirted with him. It just felt like, I don't know. Innocent. We were just playing. You know?"

Nikki nods, vaguely, again.

"We were in the steam room one night, or it was, like, before dinner. Rachel's mom wasn't home. We were going to make popcorn and watch movies, me, Rachel, and Gerald. And we'd been horsing around in the ocean before. Gerald kept teasing us that he was going to untie our bathing suits. It sounds fucked up now, but then, every-thing was cool.

"It was superhot. We had towels on, me and Rachel, above our, you know, our breasts, and Gerald had his tied around his waist. And we sat across from him, and Rachel

258

had her eyes closed. But I didn't. And he was staring at me. He has these crazy blue eyes. And so, I don't know why I did this. But I said that I was so thirsty. And Rachel opened her eyes. 'Yeah, me too,' she said. And Gerald said that orange juice would taste good. And Rachel, because she was super-helpful, said she'd go get some.

"She got out. He told me to lock the door. I did. And then I sat back down. All he was doing was staring at me. That's it. He never asked me to do anything. But for some reason, I untucked my towel, and opened it up."

Nikki's eyebrows go up, and Delia's face gets mottled with embarrassment.

"What happened?" Nikki asks.

"Nothing. Rachel came back down. She tried to open the door and it was locked. I got my towel together, and opened the door. She gave me this look, like, of murder. I laughed, said we were locking her out, we were messing with her. But she sat down, icy cold, and I knew I'd so screwed up."

"Is that it, though? That's why you're here?"

"Um, *yeah*. Do you have any idea what happens when a girl spreads the word that you did something with her step-father? Do you have any sense of the shame people wanted me to feel? My best friends, even Celeste, their parents said they couldn't hang out with me. People talked about my parents, how they'd fucked up and raised us all wrong." She spits this last part: "People don't know *shit* about my family."

"All right, *easy*," Nikki says with the tiniest smile.

Delia stares at her in horror. "You are such a whore."

"Ex-*cuse* me?"

Nikki and Delia both stand up, ready to fight.

Delia points in Nikki's face: "You asked me to tell you and I did. Last year I showed some loser stepfather my tits in a fucking steam room. You asked me about Boston, and I *told* you. If you want to ask me about Teddy, I will tell you. I did nothing wrong in Boston. And I fucked up in New York. I repeat, I have never lied to you."

"Yeah, but I mean, you did fuck up in New York." Nikki's aware her voice sounds small and mean now. "I mean, Greg's my friend too."

"Oh my *God*." Delia laughs in angry, crazy exasperation. "You've been cheating on Seth since the day after you made a promise to him. And be-*sides*, you're insanely jealous of Greg. He's your *friend*? Please, you want him to find out so I don't have him anymore."

Nikki loses some momentum. "Yeah, but I told Gabriel today, I told him everything I did. Before he found out."

"You don't *GIVE A SHIT* about Gabriel. And, anyway, that is your choice," Delia hisses, and her face is now very serious. "Listen to me. I have never told you what you should do. And on top of that, I have never judged you.

You're my friend." Her eyes well up suddenly, and she has trouble getting the rest of her words out. "I do not make verdicts on you. Do you understand?"

"Friends help friends make decisions," Nikki says in her meager voice.

Delia wipes hot tears from her cheeks. She laughs in a throaty, sad way. "You're full of shit, Nicole Olivetti. And as of this moment, we are *not* friends." And she walks out the door, leaving it open.

Greg got his observatory key from the captain of the football team. It's one of the hardest keys on campus to get. He's not there when Delia gets there, and she waits outside. Suddenly he blooms out of the dark and kisses her cheek as he unlocks the door.

"Sorry I kept you waiting, Deals."

"It's okay," she says quietly. She's in a strange, Zen way. Uncertain if she'll spill the beans and lose him, or lie and keep him.

They blunder into the dark room. The telescope is computer controlled, and it's off, so when Delia looks, she sees nothing. But through the vent in the roof, as Delia and Greg lie on the floor, they stare at a million stars and the rosy half-moon too.

"Please don't run away again," he says.

She shakes her head that she won't and inhales. It's him,

it's Greg: cocoa butter, fabric softener, African musk oil that he buys on the street in Brooklyn.

"What did you do?" he asks in an even tone.

"Nikki wanted to see Seth, and then Sunday night, that was the fucked-up night. We got off the train on our way back here, and drank at this dive and then stayed at a Motel Six. It was retarded. Baby, it was so stupid." She huddles in his arms, aware—from hearing herself say the words—that it really had been dangerous, idiotic.

But Greg is suddenly laughing, rolling on the floor. "Are you for *real*?" he asks, gasping. "Oh, shit, that is crazy! You girls are insane. That is *awesome*."

His brassy laugh boomerangs around the spherical room, and he cuddles her, tickling her, and she has to laugh. She tickles him back, under the stars, and suddenly they're kissing, and falling into space, spiraling in love. And the moment that she was going to tell him shoots through the night, sizzling, fading, dying. *Teddy's dead. Teddy never was.*

All's fair in love and war.

The school has tipped like the *Titanic*, into final exam week, spilling everyone into misery and attempts at survival. The ice one day started melting, and trees and buildings rained. The whole day was a steady drip-drip-drop of melting ice.

During the past week and a half, Nikki avoids Delia,

which isn't hard to do because Delia avoids Nikki. But Nikki feels queasy, off-kilter, since they talked.

Upper-forms are crazy about these final exams. Some parents even rented them hotel rooms in town so they could be alone to study. There's psychosis on the grounds, as kids cross paths, murmuring facts: They're soldiers of world wars, halos of atoms ringing their sweaty foreheads, speaking Shakespearean English.

Nikki wills herself to study, to write her papers. She thinks back to who she was one year ago, watching these kids around her using couture study methods learned from tutors and special programs. All she knew to do was drink black coffee, bum Ritalin, and beat her brain into submission. She'd barely gotten by. Now she and Parker have a study haven, with green tea and Philip Glass and breaks every forty-five minutes to quiz each other. Parker's sprawled, in black jeans and a red wifebeater, reading her art history textbook and making calligraphic notes in the margin.

"You doing all right?" Parker asks without looking up.

"Yeah, you?"

"Eh," Parker says, a cap in between her teeth as she squeakily highlights a line.

It doesn't add up, Nikki thinks as she looks at the wet landscape. This year of seventeen. The serious year. Gabriel won't look at her. Somerset sent her suggestions neatly handwritten on his stationery for her next advisor. Just yesterday, she'd been talking to one of the Preps who was his advisee too. He'd mentioned going to the movies with Somerset. Turns out Somerset took everyone to the movies.

On the phone last night, she asked Seth why Delia left La Jolla. Just to see what he would say. He told her that the town was too small for someone like Delia. "It can be fucking petty there," he said, which tweaked Nikki's conscience. Seth misses Nikki, and they talked about his Long Island trip at Christmas. The blue lights on the tree, tinsel strung on the branches. The rottweiler nestled with the Maltese. Sharon pouring Seth red wine while Vic grills him in the white-carpeted living room. A house party in Amityville. Spaghetti in Queens.

"What's wrong?" he asked her at one point.

"Oh, nothing," she said. "Why?"

"You seem distracted."

Delia came down the aisle of chapel today, as everyone left in order, and Nikki waited to make eye contact. Delia walked with her back straight and head high, in her red wool sweater and khakis. A beach girl in an increasingly cold winter up north.

Seventeen. The season for being accountable. What happens now? Because Nikki knows she wasn't right. She and Delia are alike. Two girls who get judged. Two girls who stand straight.

Nikki gets up. Parker asks where she's going.

"Just downstairs for a sec."

Delia answers her door in yoga pants and a Shetland sweater and bare feet. She doesn't say anything to Nikki, but leaves the door open and sits back on her bed. *Exile on Main St.* is playing loudly, and Delia doesn't turn it down.

"Deals," Nikki begins. Then she looks at the stereo. "Can I turn this down?"

Delia shrugs.

Nikki sits on the floor. "I'm a hypocrite."

Delia looks at her. In her mind, she sees the whole of the friendship. The bonfire sparks last summer. The aquamarine mist at the rope swing. Smoking, not smoking. Apple picking. Doing each other's nails in cherry red. The ebony river in Boston. Snow. Ice. That red neon sign that said BAR. And two beams of light coming into their faces.

"You have to make a decision, Nik."

"I will never judge you."

Delia picks at her nail, looking at it. "I'm not telling Greg about New York."

"That's fine, baby."

"Do you know what I was trying to do, in the steam room, with Gerald?"

Nikki waits for her friend to answer her own question.

"I was trying to block out his own stepdaughter, his wife. I was trying to be more important and more beautiful than anyone he knew."

Nikki nods. "I understand."

The evening becomes blue with snow. Exams come and go. Papers get written, rewritten, revised, revised again, reread. *Click-click-click*, the students sit and stand, like mechanized toys.

Teams play their last games, and some go on to tournaments. The boys' hockey team gets beat at the end, and they come home with bloody chins, nicked blades, broken hearts. The vending machines run out of Red Bull. No one does laundry. No one calls home. Life is on hold.

After cleaning out her gym locker, Delia sees a sign for a free swim period in the indoor Olympic pool. That sounds good. She has one more exam, but goes anyway. When she gets to the pool, no one's there. The water sends up wisps of vapor, and the chlorine is powerful, singeing her throat when she breathes. Delia drops her towel and climbs down the silver ladder.

She sinks, feeling her hair soak up the water, and then rises. Languorously sidestrokes. Floating in the mist.

And a new creed crystallizes in her mind.

This is what you do. You feel low, you stand tall. You mess up, you move on. You want to try something, try it, and if it was a stupid thing to try, you look it in the eye. There's no turning back. You apologize if you're sorry, but know that the nimblest, strongest hands can't rebuild a bridge out of embers, so cut new wood. Start from scratch.

You love with your whole heart. If you're jealous, talk yourself down from the ledge. If you can't talk yourself down from the ledge, have a good time up there, looking down on the world. If you have to lie to make everything true again, lie like you mean it. If you find yourself in a cage, reach out through the bars for the key, unlock the door, and run away. If running away gets dangerous, run home. If home doesn't mean what it used to mean, decide what home will be in the future.

If your best friend says she doesn't trust you, hold her jaw in your hand until it hurts, and make her face you. That's all it takes. If you think you love a guy, see how his hand looks in yours. That's all it takes.

If you get exiled into a new land, then go discover it. And if you feel like you're drowning, go swimming.

Don't miss next semester:

CRASH TEST

AN UPPER CLASS NOVEL

Parker's semester doesn't open with a bang. It opens with a bit of blood.

Her bags are still packed. She didn't have the heart to drag out the books and wool sweaters and vintage T-shirts and notebooks, and commit them to that room again.

Instead, she stands in Happer woods, picking tobacco from her lip as she smokes. Gray—that castle of girls—looms on the hill, its golden windows like eyes. Although in truth, she can't be seen. One just *feels* watched on this campus.

She adjusts the fur hat over her ears. It's a lot of things out here—white, dark, wide, empty, starry—but it's not warm. On her floor, girls are probably making hot chocolate in their pajamas, gossiping. The house of sisters is giddy to be reunited.

Nikki and Delia seem resigned to be back. Nikki's still a hundred-percent Long Island, in oversized Gucci sunglasses and a French manicure and Juicy Couture hoodie. She's healthier than when she arrived last year, toned and rosy from chopping and planting on Woods Crew. And wiser. Delia's gained a few pounds, from late-night pizza and vinegar potato chips, and is growing dreads. But she hasn't lost her California gold-dust shimmer.

And, Delia and Nikki each have the North Star of being in love. Nikki has Seth, even if he's in New York, and Delia has Greg. Parker has a guiding light, too: Chase. But she navigates by hating him.

"Shit." She smokes in the dark.

Chase. *Ugh.* Everything she loved—the devil-may-care snarl, the pretty boy face, doe eyes that go dark when he's bored or jealous, the swagger of a younger brother forever bullied. His slouch says: *I'll stay here or go where I want, thank you very much.* These things are reversed, like a negative photograph. All that was love now equals hatred.

These black woods are still, and wetness creeps up her blue jeans. She thinks she sees eyes in the bramble. Okay. Now she's really cold. And she's pushing Check In. She stomps the butt out and looks at the imaginary eyes.

They close.

She loses her breath.

She starts walking to the vision. The body. And there's a whine. She gets close enough to see; it's a dog. Laid up against a fallen tree. She strikes her Zippo: blood on the snow. He bares his teeth.

She lets the flame go out. Her heart is pounding.

"Hey there," she murmurs.

His gums shine as he growls.

"Hey, love. I'm not going to hurt you."

His eyes shut. He's too tired to fight, or he's giving up.

"Oh God," she frets. "Hang on."

Gingerly, she stoops over him. One eye opens—barely—and the lid drops. His lips hang. His teeth are pink with blood. Her hands are shaking—from cold and fear—and she holds one to his nose to sniff. A mortal courtesy. He does not react.

And so she goes further, and wedges her fingers under him. He's not warm. His nose twitches and black lips quiver. But he either doesn't have the heart to battle or he succumbs because this is the only chance.

He's a small, dense dog, like a cow hound. She holds him to her chest like a sleeping five-year-old, struggling with his weight, and walks as briskly as possible on snowed-over roots. Emerges from the woods and hikes up the incline, breath like blue smoke, toward the gold lights. She's heaving by the time she gets to Gray.

"Hey!" she yells at the stone building.

Katie Liesl comes to the door, toothbrush in hand. Her eyes widen, taking in the injured animal.

"Get Mrs. Jenkins," Parker says.

Mrs. Jenkins, the housemaster, and Parker drive to the animal hospital—snow pushed to the shoulder—farmhouses sliding by. Parker calls the hospital on Mrs. Jenkins's phone, gets a groggy woman. They pull into a lot, one light shining on the cinderblock building. A woman with a bun stands at the open door, her white sleeves shivering. She comes to them with an animal stretcher, leans it against the car.

"Is he yours?" she asks.

"I found him in the woods. I think he's dying."

The vet touches the dog's throat. She doesn't say anything.

Mrs. Jenkins and Parker hold ends of the stretcher while the vet takes the dog in an embrace, and transfers him. Immediately the stretcher's white canvas starts to absorb a splotch of red. Now the vet holds the door and directs them to a room. In the clinical light, Parker looks at this animal—beautiful and ruined. His eyes, blue slits under black rims. His hide is speckled like tortoiseshell.

"Let's see what's going on," the vet says, feeling his body with gloved hands.

She gets a weak snarl as she tests his back leg.

Parker feels tears well up. "Is he going to be okay?"

The vet continues examining him. Then she looks at Parker. "I'm not sure. He's in shock."

"Did he get hit by a car?" Mrs. Jenkins asks, her brow furrowed.

The vet takes off her gloves and leans against the metal counter. "I think he was probably beaten, then thrown onto the highway or something like that. He's just a pup. Must have been too many in the litter. Happens all the time. If you look at his face and back, he's got scars. It looks like he's been through it. I'm going to keep him overnight, obviously. Let me see what I can do." The vet speaks kindly but firmly, unwilling to make promises, unwilling to make excuses for the laws of nature.

Parker cries most of the way home. Mrs. Jenkins lets her. She keeps looking at Parker, then at the road. When Parker's sobs have lessened, Mrs. Jenkins smiles.

"Strange way to start the semester, isn't it?" Mrs. Jenkins says dryly.

Parker can't help but laugh. She wipes her eyes. Her sleeves are stained with blood. Yes, it is a strange beginning.

Second week of school. Airplanes cross the frozen aquamarine sky. Students wear duckboots, the hoods of their jackets pulled over their faces.

Laine has somehow landed in the Girls Varsity Ice Hockey try-outs. She's here partly at the urging of her therapist, Anne, who wants her to try new things. Laine's been seeing Anne since she got back to Wellington after the 60 Thompson nightmare, and finally it looks like Laine's moving beyond the nosebleeds and compulsive running and midnight puking and the need to say the right things or nothing at all.

And Dr. Puretzky coaxed her here. *Your stick skills, your athletic ability, you sense of the game—you're going to be first line, Laine. You just have to learn how to skate.*

Ha! she thinks. *Just have to learn how to skate.* The ice stretches like an impossibility. From rafters, pennants sway. Everything echoes—especially Dr. P's whistle when he signals the girls to race to the sideboards. *Here we go.*

Laine's arms flail like chicken wings as she works across the rink. The other girls glide, arms swinging, touching the boards and making sweeping turns. Laine crashes into the boards, and makes the clumsy journey back. She's heaving, and red.

Dr. P blows his whistle for the other girls to take laps and he stands with Laine.

"Good job, Lainer."

She looks at him with sarcasm in her blue eyes. "Yeah, right."

"I'm serious," he assures her. "You gotta start somewhere. Now let me show you something."

"Okay," she says, lifting the front visor of her helmet.

He crouches on his skates. He smacks his thighs like

meat. "The key to good skating is being grounded. Get down like this, in a chair-sitting position."

She bends her knees.

"Yeah, that's it. If you stand tall, you get knocked down."

Next he shows her how to push out of sitting, shoving each skate away by the inner blade.

She sits deep, then pushes one skate left and the other right. And her body feels it, like a key clicking in a lock. *This is how you do it.* Just then, her blade catches a crevice, and she takes a digger. Spins on the ice. Even getting up is a debasement, and she kneels like a child, pushing herself up with her stick, falling, and then standing.

From the bleachers, Noah and two other Varsity guys are watching. His black North Face jacket unzipped, cheeks rosy. God, he used to think Laine was "pretty." Just "pretty." Now he can't take his eyes off her.

"That's the way!" Noah shouts, unable to keep quiet.

Oh, how dare he watch me, she thinks. Laine *is* learning not to obsess over perfection. But not when Noah Michonne is watching! It's not like she *likes him* likes him. But she doesn't need his long face and black wavy hair and deep eyes turned in her direction. This isn't the first time, either, this week that she's felt his eyes on her. Whenever guys observe her, she can't help but feel like meat in a butcher case, trussed with string.

In the locker room, she steps into the shower. Lets water

stream over her. Laine has stellar genes, Mayflower DNA. Her dad's dad married a Swede, injecting angelic, wintery beauty into the sometimes dumpy, hard-jawed WASP stock. Laine was magnificent from birth, with Mediterranean-blue eyes and white-blond hair. But she's not assured of this, and doesn't know how to use it. In her dark hours, it doesn't save her. It's amazing how many times a day she still tumbles into the belief that she's not good enough. That she'll never be good enough.

That first month of school is evil cold. New classes, new teachers, sussing out new crushes in new classrooms. Chase heads out of his dorm into the white world in Ray-Bans and a camel-hair coat, with his morning Red Bull. Sleep crystals caked in the corners of his eyes.

Summer is the loser dorm, where Chase was placed to keep him from making trouble in fertile territories. Nerds are now returning from classes or spilling out of the building, with their graph-paper pads and sci-fi fantasies and unpopped zits.

"What's up, bro?" asks Levi, in his enthusiastic Lower-form way.

"Calm down," Chase answers as they cross paths.

Chase's drawl has only increased, as though he's hanging on to a world—of sweet tea and Cajun catfish and red sunsets and low country and shrimping boats. This January air can't freeze his heritage out of him.

Dr. Puretzky's Intro to Film has a long wait list but Chase got in; someone dropped out and he got a note in his box yesterday. Chase sits at the round table. Dr. P looks like Dustin Hoffman, and his New York accent is strong. His hands are bear paws. He's scribbling on the board, and chalk motes hang in the sun rays.

Parker walks in with Nikki.

Chase looks at her with a wry face: *of course she'd show up in the one class I might enjoy.* In her white coat and fur hat, she returns the same expression.

"Okay, class. Let's not waste time."

Nikki and Parker write comments on the edges of their pages for each other. The way they avoid looking at Chase confirms what they're writing. And Parker has, in fact, decided she'll pass this semester not by knitting or playing sudoku but by punishing Chase. By raking her nails down his soul. Her new hobby. Granted, he came to Canada last summer, after their falling out. But she believes it was guilt motivating him north. Last semester, he could have made things up to her a million ways, and he tried not one.

"We've got fifteen masterpieces on our plate," Dr. P says.

He goes over the syllabus, naming Charlie Chaplin's *The Kid*, and Kurosawa's *Ran*, and Scorsese's *Mean Streets*, among others. Chase tries to lose himself in this decadent list. When the bell finally rings, Chase shrugs on his coat, puts on sunglasses, and slides past Parker and Nikki.

"Hello, dumbass," Nikki says sweetly.

He puts a hand up, makes a sarcastic smile, and moves around them. When he looks back, Parker is shaking her head at Nikki, who's shaking her head back. *Girls.*

That girl. Noah is more pleased with his draw of sticks. He's sitting across the table from Laine in economics, her hair tied back, cheekbones gold from Christmas vacation. She's one of those girls that doesn't mean to be beautiful. She can't help it. It's annoying.

From the overhead projector, percentages are projected onto the screen, but nothing can compete with Miss Cashmere Turtleneck. Her blue eyes are electric in the darkened room. *She better stop nibbling the goddamn pen. How come everything she does makes me horny? She could smell her own feet at the dinner table and I'd ask for whatever she's having.* It still doesn't make sense to Noah. Last semester they were barely buddies. Now he can't stop thinking about her. It's the way of boarding schools; a month of vacation and everyone starts over.

When the lights come on, Noah grabs his books, catches up to her. *Shit, now it's time to act.* They walk toward the clang of the dining hall, not quite together but not apart.

"Hey, good job on the ice the other day," Noah tries.

Laine halts. "Are you trying to further embarrass me?"

He holds up a hand in defense. "No, dude. Honest. It was cute."

Her cheeks turn pink, and she thrusts her chin forward. "Whatever."

"I'm serious!" Noah says.

"Yeah, I realize," she says.

He laughs, looks for a guy to commiserate with but there's no one. He dallies at the coat hooks in the hall's entryway so she'll be ahead in line. Noah simmers with impatience. *This should not be so freakin' difficult.* He wonders how Chase had the balls last year to just up and take Laine for himself. Noah is forever studying Chase. *Why have I always been a wingman? Why can't I step up like the others and get what I want?*

Noah was raised in Manhattan among über-wealthy kids. Maybe it's that Noah's dad is French, or that his parents are happily married, which has made the difference. Noah and his two sisters traveled the world, listening to adults talk at dinner tables without dumbing it down, walking through museums with their art-gallery-owner mother and actually looking at the paintings. Noah, Anais, and Colette were taught to be polite, curious, gregarious. While their friends clamored for Pop-Tarts, they tried goat yogurt, cactus apples, and sweetbreads. They're a stylish family; today Noah's wearing a Dries Van Noten jacket and Miu

Miu loafers. They have a few good pieces each, and take meticulous care of them. The European way. They say please and thank you. They actually mean it.

"Oh, boy," Gabriel says, of a somewhat European sensibility himself. "Another glorious meal of chicken fingers."

"Man, I might just have cereal, that stuff looks nasty."

Noah's reserved, yes, and jealous of his buddies back home who own the world. What Noah doesn't know yet is that those guys are one-trick ponies. Take Frederick. Even at four, Frederick ran his home. At dinner, his parents and their guests answered every nonsensical question of his as if he was an esteemed gentleman. His mother, who could make corporate executives cower, would not say no to Frederick. He's the king. If Noah looks closer, he'll see that all the kings he knows are turning into sociopaths. Noah should covet his own discipline, his manners, but that's a hard thing to do when you want someone as bad as he does.

As very, very bad as he does.

He looks at Laine as she inspects a plum. The shimmer of hair. The doll waist, pinched by a tweed skirt. The leather boots. Should he learn to be like other guys, and reach out and take exactly what he wants?

Noah can't shake the feeling that Laine *does* want him to pursue her. She just doesn't know it.

WELCOME TO
WELLINGTON

JUST BECAUSE YOU'RE RICH, BRILLIANT,
AND PERFECT IN EVERY WAY DOESN'T MEAN
YOU CAN SURVIVE BOARDING SCHOOL.

CHECK OUT THE FIRST TWO NOVELS IN THE UPPER CLASS SERIES!

No one ever thinks they'll crash and burn in their first semester—but someone always does.

Laine is a born Wellington girl: rich, sophisticated, blond, killer athlete. Nikki is everything a Wellington girl shouldn't be: outlandish, sexy, daughter of a Long Island new money family.

Laine and Nikki couldn't have less in common. But to survive first semester, they just may have to stick together, or risk being the first girl to go down in flames.

So you survived first semester. That doesn't mean you can relax.

Chase is this close to being expelled.

Parker is doing fine academically—it's her social life that's on probation.

When a campus tragedy and a little fate bring Chase and Parker together, Wellington finally starts to make sense to both of them. If only it wasn't so easy to mess everything up.